I0691390

LOVE IN BLACK AND WHITE
A COLLECTION OF STORIES

First Edition

Published by The Nazca Plains Corporation
Las Vegas, Nevada
2009

ISBN: 978-1-935509-25-7

Published by

The Nazca Plains Corporation ®
4640 Paradise Rd, Suite 141
Las Vegas NV 89109-8000

PUBLISHER'S NOTE
Love in Black and White is a work of fiction created wholly by *Lance Kyle*'s imagination. All characters are fictional and any resemblance to any persons living or deceased is purely by accident. No portion of this book reflects any real person or events.

Cover Photo, Memo Photography
Art Director, Blake Stephens

DEDICATION

For Mario

LOVE IN BLACK AND WHITE
A COLLECTION OF STORIES

First Edition

Lance Kyle

CONTENTS

THE VOYEUR AND THE BUSBOY

The view from the hotel window was of a parking lot just below—the row of trash cans that lined the alley behind it—the flat, asphalt top of the grimy, brown brick building behind that—and a hazy collection of steeples and grey office buildings farther on. If Edward Nelson shifted to his left he looked out on more of the same. Shifting to his right he saw the side street to his hotel, and across that street the row of storefronts behind clouded display windows. A single doorway punctuated the line of failing businesses, leading, he supposed, to the apartments behind the windows on the second and third floors of those buildings, all crammed together and leaning in on one another.

A bell chimed the hour in a distant church; checking his watch, Nelson clucked—the bell was at least a minute slow. So, six o'clock. Not too soon to go to dinner. Not too soon at all. Much better that he told the people at the school not to mind him, much better indeed. He could choose his own place to eat, didn't have to socialize. Avoid the awkwardness.

Checking his pockets carefully to make sure he had his keys, his wallet containing just enough cash for dinner, his under-the-shirt money belt

1

with the rest of his funds, he stepped into the hallway, yellow-lit from a bulb overhead, and closed the dark wooden door to his room behind him. He carefully threw the deadbolt with his key, tested it, then went to the stairs. No sense wasting electricity to take the elevator when he was just on the second floor. Waiting… nobody, no sounds, in the stairwell. Walking down quickly, holding the banister, then through the door into the small lobby and out onto the street.

Well, not THAT way…. the wino on the sidewalk decided that for him. There was a café over to the right, in the row of miserable little businesses, he'd go there. Not too expensive, clean, respectable. Just the thing. He pushed in the glass door and entered, a quick survey noting that the room was about two-thirds full—a good sign—mainly of an older crowd. Mainly singles. He smiled weakly at the waitress and followed her to a small booth by the big window in the back.

The soup and tuna sandwich combination, that should do. His wife would have encouraged a salad, but she wasn't here, now was she? He'd live dangerously. Giving back the menu, Nelson looked out the window, just making out the edge of his hotel. He was at the end of the block of stores and upper-floor apartments across the side street that could be seen from his window. If he stretched, he could make a good guess as to which of those windows was his room.

Pulling his focus back to the glass, he could just make himself out. Thirty-ish, not bad looking, rather a jaunty bow tie if he said so himself, a flop of dirty blonde hair, small round glasses. He shook his head and smiled inwardly—he really did look like an accountant, as his wife told him so often, no use denying it.

The couple in a booth near to him got up, hobbling out on canes the both of them. Nelson smiled again; would he and Doris be like that in another forty years? For a moment that space stretched ahead of him like a desert, and then he shook the treasonous thought from his mind. There was so much to be said for stability, comfort, the sure thing. That's what he had.

These musings were interrupted by the approach of another figure toward that booth. Black pants, white dress shirt opened at the collar, white apron: the busboy. Nelson saw him in profile as he cleared the dishes from the table into his tub. Black... no, actually a dark tobacco brown, a short skullcap of dense, jet black hair.... Very thin, about six feet tall, but with a high, curved, bottom that seemed to thrust out and upward, straining his black pants. Maybe twenty? Certainly no older than that. An oval face above a long, thin neck. Thick, full lips, reddish brown, almost as high as they were wide, contoured like a fat almond. A large, pear-shaped nose, deeply dark eyes and high cheekbones. He looked... he looked African, original, as if from the motherland.

Nelson realized he was staring just in time to shift his eyes away... just before the busboy cocked his head slightly and glanced over at Nelson. Then he looked back at his work, gave the table a good wipe with a clean cloth, and carried the tub back to the kitchen.

The meal came and Nelson ate it dutifully. Night began to fall outside, even though it was turning spring. There may have been something about downtowns in these grimy Northern industrial towns that trapped shadows. Other diners finished and drifted away singly or in pairs, never in groups larger than two. Nelson's eyes followed the busboy furtively as he bused each opening table. Nelson finished his meal. He courteously refused an offer for coffee or more water. He asked for the check. He paid it. He sat there, wondering why he didn't get up. So he did get up, and the busboy appeared in the aisle between the tables as he began walking out. Their eyes met for the briefest contact as they passed by in the aisle, the busboy moving to one side between the tables, the tiniest of nods between them, and then Nelson was out on the sidewalk.

There were if anything more bums on the sidewalk now, sprawling, begging, than there had been before. It was dark and a strange city. Nelson walked quickly across the street and into his hotel lobby. Checked out the stairwell, walked up quickly to the second floor, down the hall, threw the deadbolt and went into his room, deadbolting it behind him. He called his wife on the cell phone to report the highlights of the day. An auditor for the state board of education, he had made a good start on the books of one of the local high schools... although he was intrigued by a discrepancy or two in connection with the French department, but he'd sort that out over the next few days. Nelson asked his wife to give their daughters a hug, gave her a long-distance peck on the cheek, and hung up.

Another two hours passed watching public television; what a good thing that was, always reliable and educational programming in nearly every town. Then a little reading. Was he ready for bed yet? Not quite. Bored. Bored. He walked to the window and looked back out on the scene. The neon sign for his own hotel, evidently near to but a little above his own window, flashed on and off, now illuminating the scene and now darkening it. The alley below had more bums in it than it had during daylight hours, but he knew that already. Lights in the storefronts across the street were off. Above the stores on the second floor.... Above the stores most of the apartment windows had some kind of light coming from them. Most were covered with closed blinds, or drapes. But not one of them. It appeared to have no covering of any sort. The window revealed what seemed to be a very plain room, furnished with a dresser, maybe a table and single chair, and a bed. From the left of this frame walked a figure toward a door next to the dresser, evidently a closet, opened it, and went in.

Nelson's attention was suddenly hooked. Was that...was it the busboy? Was that possible? He stared intently at the closet door. The figure came out and closed the door behind him. Yes, it was! He had evidently hung up his work clothes carefully and was wearing only briefs.... skimpy briefs, sort of a speedo style. He disappeared out of the left of the frame for a moment, then came back with a sack which he put on the table. Opening it he removed something...evidently food, spread it on the table, then sat down to eat.

What a coincidence! But then Nelson reconsidered and decided it was not so strange. The busboy might well look for housing near his place of employment. Nelson had gone to the nearest café, so whomever he found working there might well be living nearby.

Nelson couldn't look away. The young man at the table was in profile, and not far from the window. As he ate, he looked out of the window from time to time. Suddenly, Nelson realized that he might be seen. Moving back quickly, he looked around. First, he took from his suitcase a pair of binoculars—so handy in case a good birdwatching opportunity presented itself on one of his assignments. Then he turned off all the lights in the room and stealthily returned to the window. Focusing the binoculars, the young man at the table came into view. So did the faded floral pattern on the wallpaper, the utter simplicity of the room, the thin spread on the bed by the wall.

Moving back to the man, Nelson saw that he was finishing his meal. He rose; his body was indeed thin, but not gaunt, just skinny, and a deep tobacco brown all over. His hard bottom pushed the speedos out and up in the back. The busboy's figure moved out of the frame to the left again, was gone for a moment...Nelson began to feel disappointment... and then returned. The busboy spread what seemed to be books and paper on the table and sat down again, working on them for what seemed like half an hour. Nelson stood there the whole time, looking through the binoculars, his imagination filling in the parts of the scene he could not see.

Now the busboy closed the books and shuffled the papers into a stack and rose. Moving away from the table, he stood right in the window looking out on the street. Did he not fear being seen, standing there in his skimpy briefs? But then it occurred to Nelson that his hotel did not appear to have a high rate of occupancy, there were no other open businesses in the block, the winos wouldn't care, and he... he himself could not be seen, standing in the dark of his room. The busboy stood at the window and looked out. Nelson's heart beat in time to the flashing of the hotel's neon sign outside. Then the busboy turned away again, disappeared for a moment. The room went dark; evidently he had flicked a switch. Nelson could just make out the movement of a dark body in the dark, in the general direction of where the bed stood... and then all was still.

Nelson realized that he was tense, sweat trickling from his armpits— but why? A man who was paid to find out answers to mysteries of bookkeeping, he now analyzed himself. Was he...could he be attracted to the fellow? There had been a couple of experiences in his boyhood, that one drunken debauch in college, but no really serious same-sex contacts, nothing more than was normal, as he knew well from reading, and yet—he couldn't deny the slight wetness against his underwear that he now felt. Horror warred with desire. He had always...well no, tell the truth, he had mainly been faithful to his wife. An accountant on the road is subjected to so many temptations, and he had succumbed once or twice to an alluring female principal.

Well, it was over now. Shedding his clothing, going to the bathroom once more, Nelson slipped into bed. It had been a long day, and soon he slept.

The next day's work was steady and satisfying. The discrepancy in the French department he had traced to the French Club, but he thought it was likely a case of simple mismanagement and not anything criminal. So important to maintain proper procedure, he'd be sure to offer some advice on the matter when he left. His local contact dropped him off at the hotel—Nelson had passed on an offer to join some of the high school staff for drinks. Back in his room, the door securely locked, Nelson found himself looking forward to dinner. It was ten till six when he clicked the lock in the door behind him and padded down the threadbare hall carpet toward the stairwell. Down the stairs, down the street, and back into the café at the end of the block.

He asked the waitress for a table at the back, so he could have a good view of the whole restaurant. This time he ordered soup, sandwich, AND salad... it might take him a good fifteen minutes longer to eat such a meal. The early diners, evidently all of them retirees, began finishing and leaving even before his own food arrived. As each finished, the busboy came out with his tub.

Nelson planned his surveillance very carefully, turning his head at an angle so that if discovered he could quickly shift his eyes straight ahead and not appear to have been looking at the youth. The busboy's thin figure moved with a kind of grace among the dirty dishes, the darkness of his skin visible underneath the whiteness of his dress shirt. It was clear he wore no undershirt. Nelson, having seen most of what was beneath the clothing, could now better imagine the youth's muscular, slim body moving beneath the fabric.

His meal arrived and the tables achieved a sort of stability; nobody was finishing just yet. Most of the tables were full, of older people again. A hunk of Nelson's sandwich disintegrated onto his plate, diverting his attention to scooping it back up. When his eyes rose, there was the busboy, coming toward him with a pitcher of water.

The youth smiled faintly and asked, "More water, sir?" The busboy had an accent, sort of a British Empire lilt. Nelson smiled back and nodded, saying "Yes, thank you." A tobacco brown hand moved the pitcher down to the glass in front of him, allowing Nelson to observe it closely, seeing the darker seams where the skin was creased or folded in the knuckles, the lighter tan of the palms. "Thank... thank you," Nelson stammered and the busboy smiled again as he moved off to fill other water glasses.

Nelson absently ate the rest of his meal and realized that his heart was beating a little faster than usual. He sipped some water. Then sipped some more, than drained the glass. His eyes tracked the busboy's movements, now clearing off a table. When the waitress came, Nelson would have to ask for the check. But the busboy came first, back with water. "More water, sir?" The accent was Oxford by way of.... where, the Islands? Kenya? "Yes, please," said Nelson, passing the glass to him. Their fingers brushed as the busboy took it from him, smiling, and Nelson's heart thumped. Summoning his courage, he spoke: "A busy night tonight!" The busboy smiled again, "Yes, sir," put the water glass back down and was off. The waitress with the check appeared instantly, and Nelson's departure could not reasonably be delayed.

Back in his hotel room, Nelson watched television in the dark, going to the window every ten minutes to see if the light in the apartment window across the side street had come back on. "This is pathetic," he told himself fiercely, more than once, but he could not help it. Looking into that bare apartment had become like a drug to him. Up and down, checking, every ten minutes. The trip to the window that showed him the new rectangle of light across the street made his heart thump. Nelson rushed to turn off the television and seize his binoculars.

In the frame of the window, the busboy moved from the left again but this time with a towel wrapped around his waist; had he been showering? The youth carried another sack of food which he spread out on the table and ate. Like a wolf of the air, Nelson stalked every move with his binoculars, as the lightning flash of the neon sign lit up the forest of the city in steady rhythm. The youth finished his meal and once again moved out of the frame to discard the food and bring back books and paper. More work on those items for perhaps half an hour, and then the youth came to the window and looked out.

He stood there for long minutes, looking out, seeming to find something in the dark to occupy his attention. Nelson scanned the youth's torso above the towel, seeing (or imagining when he could not see) thin but taut muscles on his chest and abdomen. Then the youth looked down and seemed to pick at his towel, tugging at it. With a single, quick movement the youth undid it and refastened it, really too quickly for Nelson to focus on anything but a flash of dark tobacco skin behind the white of the towel. The youth then moved out of the frame of the window and the light went out. This time Nelson could track his movement to the bed, as the white towel was faintly visible. Then the towel moved and fell, and a dark shape folded into the general area of the bed.

It was over. Nelson's heart was beating, and sweat again trickled from his armpits but also in his groin and down his thigh, mixing with a thin discharge of clear liquid from his penis. Unable to understand his own behavior, Nelson shook his head to clear it, put the binoculars away, and retired to his own bed as quickly as he could.

There was great progress the next day in the audit. The staff at the high school was cordial to Nelson, but had ceased offering to entertain him in the evenings; it was clear he wanted to be alone. At the end of the day, Nelson shuffled his papers back together into his valise and was driven back to the hotel. Up the stairs quickly to his room, a quick washup, and down the stairs to the café by five thirty.

The waitresses now recognized him by sight. So did the busboy, who nodded and smiled as he made his rounds; this early he was not clearing away many tables but was refilling water glasses instead. Nelson drank like a camel at an oasis. He ordered what he had eaten the night before, completely uninterested in what was put before him. He was there to track the busboy like a hawk.

The youth came by for a first water refill. Knowing it would mean a brushing of hands, Nelson handed him the glass and as it was being refilled he pushed himself to ask, "Where are you from?" The busboy smiled politely and replied. "Congo... the Democratic Republic of the Congo, to be exact, as it is now called." He put the filled glass back on the table and looked at Nelson to see whether there would be any recognition in his face of that name. "Used to be Zaire," said Nelson. The busboy broke into a huge smile and nodded. "Yes, not everyone knows that. Yes, used to be Zaire." Nelson nodded and then asked, "Are you escaping the war?" The youth's smile faded a bit as his eyes shifted into a focus on the middle distance. "Yes," he said, then flashed another smile and moved off on his duties. Nelson's hand shook a bit as he reached for the water.

He stretched his meal out as long as he could, punctuated by the regular passes of the busboy with water or to clear nearby tables. When the time came to go, the youth was out of sight in the kitchen, regrettably. Nelson slipped out and down the block to his hotel.

The evening dragged by as the sky darkened. Nelson did not look out the window as often; it was clear nobody would be there until later. About the time that the busboy might be arriving, he began looking every five minutes, and again his heart flipped when the window was illuminated across the way. Once again, Nelson scurried around to put out all his own lights and to seize his binoculars.

The youth was wearing his towel again, and repeated the pattern of the previous two evenings. He finished with his books and stacked them tidily with the papers.... but no, he kept a piece or two of the paper. The youth walked to the window to look out, standing quietly surveying the scene. Nelson monitored him through binoculars. Then the young man moved the two pieces of paper to the window and splayed them out against the glass, holding them there with the palms of his hands. Nelson focused on the paper. His heart froze. The papers had two words on them: COME OVER.

Nelson wheeled back out of sight, slamming himself against the wall beside his window. Was the message for him? How could the youth know? What did it mean? Slowly, slowly he craned his head back around. The busboy was still standing there, holding up the sign. Then he lowered the papers and walked away from the window to sit at the table again.... to sit there waiting.

His heart was beating rapidly, his forehead spotted in beads of sweat, his breathing tight...what should he do? Respectability, restraint, playing it safe on the one hand....all that warred with strong desire, with an aching sense of an opportunity that might come only once in a lifetime. Would it be safe? Would he be assaulted? The busboy seemed so nice... it didn't seem as if anybody else were in the apartment. Nelson paced back and forth frantically, stopping to stare out the window each time he passed; the youth remained there, waiting. But for how long?

Shaking his head—sure it was a mistake—Nelson grabbed his keys, leaving his wallet behind cautiously, in case he were being set up. Out the door, a trembling hand turning the deadbolt lock, then flying down the stairs (no checking to make sure it was empty) and out onto the night street. Looking up he saw the window, still a shining rectangle against the dark front of the building. Where was the door? Here, it must be this one. He tried the handle and it opened onto a tiny square of cracked tile floor with mailboxes in the wall, and an inner glass door. He tried that handle and it opened as well—no security system here!— onto a flight of old, worn, wooden steps that went straight up to a hallway barely illuminated by a single, low wattage bulb in the ceiling. The stairwell smelled of cooked cabbage. His courage faltered for a moment—he could end this all now, never go back to that restaurant— but he willed his legs to move, and up the steps he went.

At the top…it must be to the right. It must be this very door. What if it were the wrong one? He'd say he had been looking for someone, invent some false name. His hand came up, then back down, then formed a fist and back up to knock, then back down again. And then the door opened a crack. An eye peered through the slit. It closed, the sound of a chain rattling, and the door opened again. "Come in," said the youth, who was standing mostly out of sight behind the door.

Trembling, Nelson entered and fought down a moment of panic when the door closed behind him. There stood the busboy, a towel still wrapped around him, hands on hips, head cocked to one side, smiling at him. His body was very slim, thin pads of muscle on his dark brown chest, just a hint of a six-pack on his abdomen. A few pearls of water from his shower still shone in his close-cropped kinky hair. Words and action failed Nelson altogether.

"I saw you. I saw you looking. All three nights, man!" the youth said in his soft, British lilt. Nelson hung his head. "I'm sorry, I didn't mean to, really I…how did you see me?" he asked, in wonder.

"Come," said the youth, and stepped to the window. Nelson followed and stood there with him, looking across the street at the second floor of the hotel where, every time the neon light flashed, the interior of a darkened room was illuminated. Nelson blushed scarlet, knowing that he had been fully visible during those flashes. "I...I am really very sorry, it was rude. I...I should leave now," he said.

"Why, you just got here!" said the youth, laughing softly. Nelson hung his head again, utterly at a loss as to what to do. "My name is Mukube," said the youth, extending his hand. Nelson looked at it, at Mukube, and then took the hand, shaking it. "Edward," he said. They held the connection between their two hands.

"So, Mr. Edward, what are you doing in the hotel over there, in this city?"

"I am an auditor...I am auditing the books of the high school," he said. Mukube nodded. "What...what are you doing here?" Nelson asked—it sounded stupid, like party chatter, but he had no idea what else to say.

"I am going to school at the university, just finishing my freshman year. I am, as you said in the café, escaping the war. I got a special visa. If I go back, I get killed," he said starkly. This hard truth penetrated through Nelson's confusion and worry; concern for the youth's wellbeing took its place. But then Mukube asked the key question: "So, Mr. Edward.... why were you looking at me?"

Nelson blushed scarlet and let Mukube's hand go. A dozen excuses flashed through his mind, each more preposterous than the one before. In despair, he told the truth: "I....I liked looking at you. I found you attractive." There was a pause. "I think I've made a mistake, I'd better go." He turned toward the door, but Mukube was there before him and put a hand on the scarred wooden panels.

"Don't go," he said. "Thank you...for saying that. It has been hard to meet people here, for me. To meet men...safely." Now Mukube seemed to hesitate. In a very small voice he asked, "Do you...do you want to stay here a while?" He raised his other hand to Nelson's shoulder, then slid it up his neck to place it gently on the side of his face. Nelson simply melted inside, leaned slightly into Mukube's cupped palm, closed his eyes and nodded his head, swallowing hard. Mukube moved his hand from the door to the light switch and turned it off. "Come," he said, taking Nelson's hand in his and leading him toward the bed.

His eyes adjusted to the dark in the few steps it took to reach the side of the bed, and Nelson could see that a fair bit of light came into the curtainless room from the street lamps and the moon. Mukube stopped and reached for Nelson's other hand, holding both of them for a moment, looking into the eyes of the white man. Then he leaned forward and kissed him lightly. He might just as well have hit Nelson with a baseball bat, for that was all it took. In two heartbeats Nelson sighed heavily, then slid his hands up from Mukube's grasp to wrap them gently around the black man's smooth, hard back, feeling the soft, silky warm skin and the thin but firm muscles beneath. The two men pulled each other in, lips meeting. Nelson was lost in the passion of the moment, sucking first one and then another of Mukube's full, luscious lips, his own lips being pulled in turn into the black man's mouth, tongues sliding against each other.

Mukube pushed Nelson back half a step and began rapidly unbuttoning his shirt; the white man could see that the dark fingers were trembling and so he assisted the process, but his own hands were hardly less steady. Nelson tugged down his own trousers, kicking them to the side, his loafers following, as the shirt came off through Mukube's efforts. The two now embraced each other again, Mukube running his palms over Nelson's back, sliding them up to his shoulders and down his biceps, while Nelson slid his fingers under the towel to dig his nails into the tight, high bottom. That made the towel fall off and Nelson could feel a thick, heavy organ slap against his thigh. Pulling down his own underwear he mashed his groin forward. Standing, pushing into each other with the force of their legs, the two men fought a war of passion. Then Nelson stepped back, his rigid penis springing up from beneath a bush of dirty blonde hair.

Mukube's own pendulous organ was heavier and longer than Nelson's, but not comic-book huge. The white man grasped the organ, purple black in the dim light of the room, and slid his hand up and down it. Mukube threw his head back and moaned loudly, a sound of release as much as ecstasy. He slid his dark brown hand down around the white man's ballsack, then around it and onto the rigid, red shaft. The two stood there for a moment like that, manipulating each other's rigid cocks, the dickheads becoming coated with a slick film of precum. Then Mukube slid down to the bed, stretching himself out, and pulling Nelson down onto him.

Stretching out on top of the dark body, Nelson cupped the man's thick skullcap of dense, kinky hair with both hands. He could have done that all night, so delicious was the feel of the crisp hair. They kissed again, kissed noses and eyes, mouths nibbled ears and gently bit necks. All the while Nelson humped the man beneath him, sliding his penis up and down on the slick brown belly while Mukube pushed upward with his hips, sliding his rigid cock up between the upper thighs of Nelson and following a rhythm of passion up and down, up and down, the reddish brown head of his dick poking up and down above the back of the white man's thighs. Mukube clasped his dark arms and hands around Nelson's back, while the white man fondled the rounded muscles of Mukube's shoulders and biceps.

Two passions merged together, born of loneliness and denial and restraint. Humping, sliding, kissing, a convulsion was born deep in the gut of each man, and quickly moved toward an explosion. Pulling his lips away from Mukube's mouth, Nelson roared, clenching and bucking frantically, his rigid penis shooting ropes of semen between their bellies as he slid back and forth on the black man beneath him. At nearly the same time Mukube's torso curled and tightened and his hips pushed upward. His dickhead poked up between the white man's thighs and shot a fountain of semen up and onto his bottom and back. Crying, gasping, clutching, the two men struggled together in that way until the storm passed. Nelson collapsed on top of Mukube, who enveloped him in his arms, clutching him tightly.

Long minutes later, Nelson rolled off to one side on the narrow bed and Mukube turned on his side with his back to the white man's belly to lie like spoons. Nelson held him tightly, out of passion but also to keep him from rolling off the bed, his arm clasping the semen-slick chest and belly, his own penis—wilting but still full—pressed between the ass checks of the prominent black butt. The two breathed more normally, and in a shared rhythm.

"Was it good?" whispered Mukube.

"It was very good. It was...it was the best. And you?" Mukube laughed deep in his throat and covered the white man's hands with his own. "It was that good also," he said.

A few more minutes of cuddling passed. Mukube spoke. "How much longer will you be in town?"

Nelson chuckled. "A while longer. I think...I think there will be some discrepancies that I will need to look into." Mukube laughed softly.

Then Nelson spoke. "You are at the university? What are you studying?"

"Mathematics."

"Really? Mathematics! what branch?" The white man's heart beat a little faster.

"Calculus."

"Calculus," repeated Nelson, stretching the word out luxuriously. "Calculus!" Not for the first time that night, and not for the last, a look of lust came into Nelson's eyes. "Mukube," he said, "I think you and I are going to be great good friends."

MARIO AND ME

I don't know how people do it who can't take a nap in the afternoon. To take a nap, you need a nice couch and a private office, of course. An office with a phone you can turn off and not answer and nobody will think that's unusual. An office where, if someone knocks on the door and you don't answer, you know they won't think it's odd and they won't try to barge in. To sum all that up, you need to be a professor.

Which I was, at a large urban public university. Now I'm at a larger, flagship university. I'm not going to say how long ago this story took place. Suffice it to say I was in early middle age (middle age, they say, but—how many 110 year old men do you know?), and HE was not.

Back to the couch; of course, if you have such a couch in such an office, it can be put to other purposes. I did so. There were several blissful/ tragic years of the relationship with the Chinese guy, the one encounter with the black guy with the scary-huge dick, the few months with the diva Malaysian guy. I guess I've always liked color more than non-color, although none of us would want to be truly "white." That would be my official description.

None of that felt like cheating on my wife. It was exercising my other half, and never interfered with a truly happy marriage. And yes, it was about half and half; can't stand gay guys who avoid dealing with it by calling themselves bi, can't stand people who think bi's are all conflicted gay guys. In my case, bi means bi, thank you very much. But this story isn't about the hetero side. It's about Mario and me.

The sauna in the men's room of the gym at the university was a good place to go fishing. It was the only place I had tried in that community. As with any fishing hole, you didn't always get a nibble, and sometimes you pull up one ugly catfish, but every now and then... This story is about something that started one of those times.

This was in July. Like many urban universities, this one had a lot of programs for inner city high school kids, which meant blacks, Latinos, some poor whites. Most of the regular students were gone for the summer, so these kids dominated the space. They would go to classes all morning, then they had gym privileges and the arena floor would be packed with a rainbow crowd from noon until mid-afternoon. High school and a few junior high school kids, the guys all playing basketball and showing off for the girls who congregated in clusters here and there, looking at the guys but trying not to look as if they were looking at the guys. The girls were hot, too, but let me not get distracted from the game board on which this story played out. You could run around the track that circled the basketball courts, pretending to watch the games, really watching the lithe young bodies sweating, moving... nearly every game was shirts and skins, and you always rooted for the skins.

It was rare, however, to see one of these kids in the showers, rarer still to find them in the sauna. Not that I didn't always look, always took longer in the shower and sauna if I knew these beauties were in the building. I always wondered what it meant to find that rare brown skinned boy sweating away in the cedar box with a bunch of white haired, white skinned professors. You often could not find out however, because the crowd would not thin out until you had to leave, or the boy had to leave, and so the question remained unexplored.

I had done my shower/sauna/shower cycle, maybe even more than once, with no luck. Not many people in that part of the building at all that day. So I was drying off in the area between the showers and sauna, getting ready to dress and leave. Around the corner from the lockers comes this guy: dark brown skin, about six feet two inches, maybe three. Close cut hair, a really handsome, open face with big eyes, full lips, broad nose (but not too broad). He's got on only this pair of cut-offs. His eyes flicker here and there surveying the scene... I'm the only guy there, the showers are otherwise empty... and he swerves gracefully into the sauna, letting the cedar door close shut behind him. OK, I had kept the whole area under surveillance, so I knew he was alone in there. I didn't want to just rush right in, especially when I had clearly been drying off. Would he notice that? Would he think about what it meant that someone dried off and THEN entered a sauna... sort of like he had other reasons for sitting around and getting hot?

At that point I still had deniability, so I didn't worry too much. I gave it a few beats, then opened the door and went in. The lights were low, but it wasn't really dark. He was sitting directly facing the door on the top shelf, and he had removed his shorts. He was completely naked on the hot cedar planks. "Hi," I said, nodding. "Hi, how's it goin'" he replied. I stepped up to the top shelf also, but to my left, so that when I sat I had a view right across him. I spread my towel on the planks and sat down.

These scenes are all the same and they're all different as we tip-toe our way toward truth or consequences: "Sure is hot in here today," I began.

"Yeah, sure is," he said. Pause.

"My name's Lance," I said, half rising and extending a hand.

"Mario," he replied, doing the same.

"Mario... that's a nice name," I said. "Were you working out?"

"Yeah, hoops."

"Oh, OK. Yeah, you look like you do work out a lot!" and here I allow myself a frank appraisal of his body. He's muscular, but not really ripped. It's as if he's had a growth spurt that outstripped some basically good development. Little hills and valleys of a 6-pack, and pads of chest muscle but nothing really outstanding. Yet still, your basic healthy, thin, athletic young black guy. His penis is large and lying straight and still between the two long hills of his thigh muscles. His arms are straight at his side, palms flat against the cedar boards, torso more or less straight.

"Yeah, HAVE to! Coach gets mad if we don't," he replied grinning widely. He began glancing quickly over at me, then straight ahead, back and forth like that.

"You play ball at school?"

"Yeah."

"Where is that?"

"North," he said, naming a local high school.

"Oh, OK... well, yeah, you sure look like you work out," I repeated. "You here for classes this summer?"

"Yeah, all morning."

"Oh, OK. So, you must be... what, eighteen?" Now, that might have been the turning point. Or was it telling him twice how much it looked as if he worked out? Or was it my steady gaze right at him? He looked straight ahead and, in retrospect, might have hung his head just a bit.

"Yeah, I'm eighteen... So," and he turned to look at me in sort of a pointed way, "you married?"

"Yeah. Got two kids." He nodded at that information. "I guess I should ask you," I said, "got a girl friend?"

"Yeah."

"Got any kids?"

He chuckled and shook his head vigorously, "Naw, nothin' like that!" More silence. One of his legs began to bounce just a little, a steady thrumming of nervous tic.

"Man, it's really hot in here," I ventured again. "You're likely to burn something sitting right there on the wood like that."

"I know it!"

"I could unfold my towel, want to share it?" That did it. There was silence, but you could hear the tumblers of the lock clicking into place.

"Uh... Naw, I'm here with a couple of friends... they might come in."

I nodded. "Well, I think I'll rinse off and come back in."

"Me, too," he said. We both left the sauna to shower. It was pretty clear to me that he had the beginnings of a hard on. We each stood at a nozzle a few feet apart, but it was also clear that we were both looking at each other pretty frankly the whole time. I turned the shower off and moved back to the sauna. He gave me a "wait a minute" sign with his hand and padded off toward the lockers. I sat back down where I was in the sauna and a few minutes later he re-entered, this time wearing his cutoffs... perhaps to hide an erection?

"Do you work out a lot?" I asked.

"Yeah, I do, every day. And hoops..."

"I guess your girlfriend must like it that you work out." He grinned and nodded. "Keeps you in good shape for sex with her, eh?" He chuckled, stretched a little, twisting his lithe young body, settled back looking at me quite directly. His leg was vibrating again. "You sure you don't want to share this towel, it's really hot," I said.

"Let me... let me see if my friends are back," he said, and left the sauna again. A couple of minutes passed, and he returned.

"I found 'em, told 'em to go without me," he said, as he sat. His leg was really bouncing now, and he kept glancing at me, then straight ahead, back and forth.

"Listen, it's really kind of hot in here anyway," I said. "I've got a private office, air conditioned, we could...talk...and not be disturbed. You want to come to my office for a soda?"

A long pause. "Uh, look, this is none of my business and I don't mean to be rude, but... are you gay?"

"I'm bi," I said. "How about you?"

"I'm bi," he said, looking straight ahead.

"Want to come to my office?" I repeated.

"Sure."

"I'll meet you in the hallway by the 'cage,'" I said. We both left the sauna again and rinsed off, this time appraising each other with full knowledge of what was about to happen. You wouldn't find him in a muscle magazine, but he was a real-world nicely built guy, well muscled... I felt lucky that things were developing this way.

What did he see when he looked over at me? This I could never figure when I landed a younger guy. I would NEVER go for somebody like me. I mean, I think I'm good looking, but I'm middle aged, a tad overweight and although I exercise every day you could never say I was muscular especially. Balding, gray hair... But I've learned not to ask that question. You never know who you are to somebody else such that they want you. Was I this guy's dad, maybe an absent dad? Was I his coach, maybe another middle aged white guy before whom he strutted naked every day after practice in the high school locker room, a guy he struggled to please and to earn the approval of? Was it my gray hair? My white skin? What was I bringing to him in exchange for his good looks, slim brown body, and youth? You just never know. Better to take the gift of the Love God and not question. And I was secretly delighted, just tickled, that this handsome young guy was willing to come to my office with me.

We met in the hallway after getting dressed, and walked almost in silence the short distance to my building. I did ask him along the way, "You ever done this before?"

"Uh... naw, just once or twice at Musclebuilders," he said naming a local gym franchise. Interesting... how much could one really do in such a public, mainstream place. It wasn't a bathhouse or anything like that. Was I getting a same sex virgin?

I took the back way in, and fortunately the hallway to my office was deserted when I let us in. I shut the door behind us and moved one of the chairs in front of it, just in case. I put a box of tissues on the coffee table in front of the couch. As I was doing that he prowled restlessly around the office, and then he saw it. The picture of my wife. Did I mention that she is black? A second marriage, much better than my first, to a white woman. He stopped dead in his tracks.

"Who is this?"

"My wife." I hadn't mentioned her color to him because it just hadn't been relevant.

He let out sort of a single, barking laugh. "Does she suck your dick?" he asked, with a new, hard edge to his voice.

"Yes, sometimes," I said. "Want to sit here?" I indicated the sofa. "Want a soda?" He nodded yes, and I got both of us one from the little refrigerator I kept in the office while he sat. I gave him his, and then sat down right next to him. We both pulled long swallows from the cans. Then I settled back and put my left arm around his shoulder and began to knead the tense muscles in the back of his neck. He closed his eyes, a couple of beats passed, and then he exploded.

Setting his can down on the coffee table, he wheeled around and over me as I sat on the couch, both legs straddling my lap and hips. Bending down he attacked my mouth with his, his tongue pushing in past my lips and gyrating furiously inside my mouth. With another hand he grabbed my crotch. I was nearly helpless under the onslaught, but I held on to his thighs and hips. In a minute he stopped and rocked back; it seemed as if he had come to the end of his plans, the last of his repertoire of foreplay, and wondered what was next. Maybe he really was new at the whole sex-with-guys thing.

"Stand up," I said, which he did. I switched off the lights in the office, then asked him to removed his shirt, which he did, standing quietly, waiting. "I'm going to give you a rubdown," I said, and moved behind him. I began kneading the warm, soft, chocolate dark skin of his neck, then the strong muscles of his shoulders. Working my way firmly but gently I passed the rounded muscles where the shoulders curve around to the arms, then the long slopes and valleys of muscles down his arm to the hard-sinewed forearms. He had that beautiful muscle contour you find in black guys, muscles just dancing and rolling with each other in perfect harmony. I tore off my shirt and came around in front. I worked the pads of muscle on his chest, definitely present but not overly developed, tweaking his nipples as I passed down across a slightly developed six pack. His navel wasn't quite an outie, but harbored a little knot of flesh considerably lighter than the sweet chocolate brown of his skin. He stood there accepting these services passively.

"Undo your pants," I said, doing the same with mine. I let mine fall, then reached to his and gently tugged down pants and underwear in one move. My average sized penis was sticking out, while his bounced out of his garments and poked straight ahead. Are black dicks bigger than white ones? Well sure, I think so. Why deny it? I can think of at least one good evolutionary reason for it, that it's a highly vascular area that disperses more heat the bigger it is, and heat dispersal is a good thing in Africa. Whereas my modest organ was designed for shriveling up in the cold winds of Germany. But that's the professor in me talking. At the moment, we were two guys with hard-ons that batted against each other. I took him into a tight embrace, but avoided kissing; his technique was just way too sloppy. I moved back around behind him and began kneading his hard butt muscles, and was starting to run my fingers into the ass crack when he whispered urgently, "Don't put your dick in my asshole."

Interesting. I was becoming more sure he was a same-sex virgin. It was real unlikely I'd just put my dick to his anus and push, both of us standing up with no lubrication or anything, but maybe he thought that was how it was done. "OK," I said, but continued kneading his high, tight, upward-rolling black-man's butt. "Um... I really just want some sucky," he said, again, nervously.

"OK," I said, "lie down," indicating the couch. He stretched out on it and I lay down on top of him, our dicks grinding together. We were both too excited for this to go on for long, and uncertain of how to make our way through this "first time with each other" territory. Soon I slid off of him onto my knees on the floor, with him laid out like a feast on the sofa before me. I kissed his chest, nibbling his nipples, then licked my way down his abdomen. I nuzzled in his nice, plush bush of pubic hair for a while, then slipped around the rampant dick to lick his scrotum. I sucked each heavy testicle into my mouth—they really were quite heavy, potent engines and full of little black baby-makers. Then back to the purple black dick, which I licked up the bottom side, tonguing the underside of the lighter reddish-brown head... and then took the whole thing into my mouth.

I pumped my head up and down as he began breathing more heavily, his hands grasping my back and one arm. The slightest up and down rhythm in his hips started to match my cadence. The penis was much too big to take in entirely, but I did what I could, and it evidently was fine with him. "Oooooo, yeah," and "do that!" and "Oh, yeah, do that thing" were repeated over and over. His rhythm increased, and then he cried out, "I'm coming." I don't know why I didn't take it then, I'd have had no objection, but it seemed as if he expected me not to, so I removed his penis from my mouth, grasped it with my hand and began pumping just as he shot out a spray of white semen all over his chest and abdomen. I slowed down as another and then another slug of cum shot out, and then it was over.

He was lying on the sofa on his back, breathing heavily, as I turned to look in his eyes. What I saw surprised me: tension, fear, maybe anger? "Listen man," he said, tightly between gasps for breath, "don't mess with me. Don't you tell nobody, for real... I'm for real, man, you just stay right here, don't do nothin' and don't go nowhere..." on and on in this way for maybe a minute. Kneeling on the floor by him still, I just looked at him. "OK," I said, laughing a little in wonder and disbelief.

"Why you laughin'?" he asked, tensely.

"I... I don't know where this is coming from," I said. "I'm not going to hurt you. Look, I like you. Nobody's going to do anything to you." It was then that I was dead certain he had never had this kind of intimacy with a man before, and that doing so had broken lots and lots of rules he had learned in his life. He had taken a plunge, and was now fearful of a host of consequences that had been whispered to him since he was a boy. "Come on," I said, "let's get dressed. Nobody's going to hurt you."

He sat up and began dressing. I gathered up pieces of our scattered clothing from the darkened office floor, handing him what was his, putting on what was mine. Putting on my shoes, I sat down on the sofa next to him, where he was nearly clothed. Then he surprised me.

"Didn't you want to come?" he asked.

"Well, yeah, but it didn't seem like you were in the mood."

"It don't matter."

"Well... I don't want you to do anything you don't want to do."

"I don't mind. It don't matter."

Nonplussed, I thought about it for a minute. Then I stood up and dropped my pants and underwear again, pulling off my shirt once more and stood right in front of him.

"Seems like you came already," he said, wiping away great gobs of precum that had gathered there. My penis had certainly wilted during the previous confusing minutes. He bent down to it and took it into his mouth, sucking it. It came right back.

I held his head in my hands, enjoying the scratchy texture of his close cut hair, fondling his small ears, as he sucked and I rocked back and forth. It was naughty of me, but I didn't tell him when I was coming, I just grunted, pushed, and started flowing. He quickly pulled his head off of my penis and wrapped his hand around it, turned his head to the right and spat my semen out on the sofa. Turning my dick in the same direction, he let it spout out its white gobs onto the same place. He kept his head turned, looking intently at the gathering islands of goo on the couch fabric. Was he seeing his first white man's semen, was he surprised that it was the same color as his?

"Was that good?" he asked, a little anxiously, when I was finished. I leaned down and kissed his forehead. "That was very good," I said. Then I dressed again and we restored the room to order.

"Well, that's was nice. I'd like to do it again some time, but it's up to you. You know where to find me," I said, feeling it was important, given his recent reticence, to leave him in control of the process... even though I wanted nothing more than to follow him home.

"OK," he said, and slipped out the door.

The next day, about the same time of day as all this occurred, I taught a summer session class down the hall from my office. "I'm in 210" I put on the door, with an arrow pointing the right way, just in case... just in case. Fortunately, I was team teaching the class. I took the first half. My colleague had begun her part of the class and I was sitting around the seminar table, facing the closed door to the room, when I saw a dark face float briefly in the wire-crossed window of the door, then disappear. "Got a student" I mouthed to my colleague, who nodded pleasantly as I moved quickly to the door.

Closing it quietly behind me, I saw Mario going down the stairs to my left. "Hi," I said.

"Oh, hi," he said, "I just stopped by. You're teaching, go ahead," he said.

"No, no, the other teacher will take over," I said. "Let's go talk."

He came back up the stairs as we walked back toward my office. "I been thinkin' about you," he said.

"Good thoughts, I hope?" I asked, putting my key in the door lock.

"Yeah, good thoughts," he said, grinning shyly, as we entered and shut the door behind us.

I stepped up to him as he stood in front of a bookcase, put one hand on his shoulder and the other around the back of his head, and kissed him. Again, he pushed a violently wagging tongue into my mouth. I pulled away gently. "Kiss slow," I said, then moved in again. He learned quickly and if to this day he is giving intense pleasure to some lucky man or woman with his kisses it is because I taught him, applause, applause.

Our kisses then and from then on were slow, measured explorations of each other, an intimate slow dance of sucking lips and tongues, pushing lips and tongues into the other to be sucked, running tongues over teeth. We were both breathing heavily through our noses, sharing breath, sharing spit. If I could have one of our moments back again, it would be one of those long kisses.

We undressed and I put him on the couch again. I stretched out on top of him and clasped both of his hands in mine, our fingers interlocking. I could see the backs of my white hands with chocolate brown fingers coming in between mine, lying across my skin, and I knew he saw a negative image of that from his side. I was pushing my chest up off of his in that way, pushing against his hands, both pairs of intertwined hands held right in front of us. I looked at them and at him looking at them. Our eyes met. We never said a word about it, but I know we both thought that was the most beautiful sight we had ever seen.

Breaking the grip, I cupped both hands around his close-cut hair. I couldn't get enough of feeling that crisp, sandpapery texture of hair as we kissed. I nibbled his nose with my lips, kissed his eyelids. Bringing my face around to the side of his head, I kissed his neck and ears. He giggled and writhed a little. "That tickles," he said. "Want me to stop?" I asked. "Yeah." He breathed. But I didn't, and he didn't ask me to stop again.

Going first this time, I stood up. He knelt on the floor in front of me, grasped my thighs, and began sucking. Again I cupped his head, finding the texture of his hair simply delicious, letting go only as I felt my orgasm approach. "I'm gonna come," I said, and he pulled his mouth off and began pumping me with his hand. When I came, it was a shower of white drops and dollops and it fell all over him as he knelt in front of me, decorating his dark chocolate skin with white medallions. Mario had the most ecstatic look on his face, as if he had just come himself. "Yeah!" he cried out, as if he had just scored a basket. I think that I need not have cleaned my semen off of his shining dark skin... I think he would have worn it like a necklace if I had not... but I did.

We switched places. It was harder for me, I think, because his penis was so much larger, but I managed. He had to say "No teeth!" a couple of times, but soon he gasped "I'm coming" and it was my turn to receive thick ropes of white semen on my shoulder, neck, and belly.

Things changed as soon as the deed was done, not as dramatically as the day before, but you could sense the difference. As we were dressing, I sensed some hurriedness in him, a need to be off. The intimacy we had just shared seemed not to last into these moments.

"Hey, do you want to exchange phone numbers?" I said.

"Naw," he replied.

"OK, do you just want my phone number?"

"Naw, that's OK. Well, I gotta go," he said, moving toward the door. I was nonplussed; I mean, we had just had our dicks in each other's mouths, and at his instigation, now he seemed eager to leave. I gently intercepted him just before he got to the door and planted a kiss on his lips. He paused, hanging his head.

"Don't fall in love with me," he said.

"Um... OK, but does that mean we can't see each other again, or maybe hang out outside this office?"

"Ah, I gotta go," he said, and was out the door.

A few days passed. I was working in my office with the door nearly closed. There was a knock, and when I opened it, there stood Mario, eyes shifting quickly as he scanned the office. "Hi, come on in," I said, and he entered, nodding. We got down to business.

Now, don't you like a little variety? Wouldn't most people? After some passionate squirming and pushing and kissing, I got up and asked him to get on his hands and knees on the floor. I got some KY I kept in the office for the purpose, and moved around behind him.

"Don't punk me!" he whispered fiercely.

"I won't, I just want to do something nice for you," I said, slicking up my thumb. I put this to his wrinkled brown asshole, which winked invitingly at me from between the two firm mounds of his butt cheeks. Mario stayed on hands and knees, but moved one hand around to clutch my wrist firmly. He was going to keep me from "punking" him, and it appeared as if that included inserting anything at all, even my thumb, into his love canal. I did what I could: scratching at it, moving my thumb in little circles at the opening, testing his limits by pushing just a little. That did it. He moved my hand away entirely, saying "I just wanna sucky."

Well, there's more than one way to skin that, cat, too. This time I laid down on the sofa and had him sixty-nine me. I was surprised that he let his precious anus float above my face so invitingly and defenselessly, but I didn't touch it again. I sucked his massive balls as they lay on my face, then pushed him up and got the end of his heavy dick into my mouth and sucked. Being on top, the action was all his. He pumped lightly while at the other end he took my penis in his mouth and bobbed his head up and down on it. I came first again, moaning to signal the impending crisis. He let it slip from his thick lips and began pumping it with his hand while I spouted all over my chest and belly. He kept that position, arched over me, bobbing his hips gently until he began to come. He pulled his own penis out and let it wag over my chest and belly as I pumped it, adding his own buckets of semen to what was already there. My torso was pretty well slicked up by the time he rolled off the couch to a standing position.

We were cleaning up when he said, "I can't come here any more."

My heart twisted. "Why?"

"Well," he said, "I gotta girl friend." I nodded; I knew he'd get over THAT. "And I'm Lutheran," he said, "and this is really bad for Lutherans." It was all I could do not to smile at him, but I didn't. "So, I can't come back."

I held him tightly, genuinely sorry to see him go. I think he hugged back, but again, it followed the general pattern of intense desire and then distance, fear, and regret afterwards. He left the office and I stood watching him go as he went down the hallway.

A month or so passed and I assumed that Mario was a thing of the past. I was in my office with the door open, talking with a former student and friend who, coincidentally, was also black. He left, and about five minutes later who should appear in the doorway but Mario.

"Someone was here earlier," he said, almost accusingly.

"Oh, Troy?" I said. "Don't worry, I've never touched him!" I said, which was true. "Um… I'm glad to see you," I said as I closed the door. "I, uh, thought you weren't coming back."

"My girlfriend and I had a fight… somethin' stooopid," he said. That seemed to explain it all for him, justified his return. Where was the church? Well, who was I to argue. We floated into another passionate session of long, exploratory kissing, hair feeling, sucking, licking, decoration of bodies with streaks of white… and the inevitable hurried, almost sullen departure at the end. "Look," I said, "it's clear you like me or you wouldn't keep coming back. I like you. Can't we just talk for a while, or go get coffee, or maybe see a movie sometime?"

"Naw, it just wouldn't work out. I gotta go to work," he said, not unkindly but with no hint of encouragement. And then he was gone.

Mario continued to appear sporadically, sometimes weeks and sometimes months apart. How often he showed up when I wasn't there, I never knew and he never said. The last time we were together I was yearning for something different, as the usual "sucky" scenario didn't allow for much variety. Lying on top of him, I pushed my erect penis down between his legs and began humping. I kissed him long and slow, cradled his crinkly skullcap, and looked deeply into his eyes as I slid in and out of his thighs. As I picked up speed and my breathing increased, he sense what was happening.

"What are you DOIN'?" he asked, breathing hard himself.

"I'm fucking you," I said. Not entirely accurate, and man was that the wrong answer. I had "punked" him. He let me come, which I did shortly thereafter, but he cleaned up and left extra fast after that.

I saw him at the gym the next summer, and once followed him down into the showers, but he was showering with shorts on and told me he had to go to work, then he left quickly. I was embarrassed for both of us. Mario had graduated from his high school and, as it turned out, went to the university—not unusual for urban kids trying to save money on room and board. I saw him sitting in a classroom a couple of times as I passed, and I made sure to pass by that way during future meetings of the class just to look in and see him. His glance flickered at me, but he made no acknowledgement. I saw him once at the gym and we actually had a pleasant but very brief conversation. I told him to come by anytime, but he didn't reply and he never did.

A better job prospect took me to another state before Mario graduated. Thank goodness for the Internet, though, for I could keep track of him in a way. I found pictures of him on a web page for a black fraternity, he was doing some service activity, standing there with other handsome black guys, a big grin on his handsome brown face. Through the university web site and through googling him I knew when he graduated with a business degree, and he even popped up as an employee on the web site of a firm doing financial services. I know his work, home, and cell numbers and at least two email addresses to try. Should I? I don't want to intrude, and I hope he's happy the way things are. Meanwhile, I've saved those fraternity pictures, and that's what I have left of him: a smiling brown eyed handsome man, frozen in time, eighteen forever.

MASTER TOM

He pulled back on the reins of his horse, squinting at the few visible wooden boards behind the tangle of bush and briar. Was this the place? Looking around him, James Thomson Callender decided that it must be, there were no other structures around that could possibly be dwelling-places. Dismounting, he tethered his horse to the trunk of a small ash tree, then pushed gingerly through the ring of patchy shrubs. Then the tumble-down house was clearly visible behind a broken wooden fence and gate, but could it possibly be occupied? There were no lights inside, even though this late spring day in 1801 was overcast and threatening rain.

The door was weatherbeaten, hardly any paint left on it. Callender knocked tentatively, then again, harder, and stepped back. He absently brushed his knuckles with a handkerchief he pulled from his pocket while he waited.

There was the sound of glass clinking inside, a thud, a chair being scraped on a wooden floor, and then footsteps—irregular footsteps. Callender took a step back as the steps approached the other side of the door. It opened a crack, revealing darkness and one bloodshot eye. Callender heard a deep sigh and some muttering, then the door opened.

There stood a stooped, disheveled, light-brown skinned man who struggled for a moment to focus on Callender, then nodded and shuffled backward, opening the door. The white man clutched his valise tighter, gulped, and stepped inside. Again he retrieved his handkerchief to hold over his nose, as a wave of whiskey stench rolled over him. He turned toward his host.

"I am James Thomson Callender," he said, then dug in his pocket to produce a grubby small rectangle of cardboard, which he held out. "Journalist," he added. "And you... sir... would be James Hemings?"

The brown skinned man swayed a little, looked at the card that Callender offered him, shrugged, croaked out a simple "Yes" and shuffled over to a small nearby wooden table. There were two wooden chairs at the table, which held a bottle and two glasses. Hemings sat down heavily in the chair, clutched the table to steady himself, then grunted and gestured toward the other chair. Callender perched on the edge of it and looked around, his eyes becoming accustomed to the gloom. Hemings was all but camping out; it was clear the building had been abandoned, and that its occupant now slept on the filthy sack of bedding in the corner. Besides the table and chairs, there was no other furniture in the room.

Callender's gaze returned to the man on the other side of the table. His age was hard to determine. Callender believed him to be about thirty-five or six based on information he had received, yet the man looked older—perhaps the effect of drink. Hemings looked at Callender looking at him, grunted again, and waved the bottle over the second glass, arching his eyebrows inquisitively.

"No, no thank you, sir," said Callender. "I... I do not wish to take up your, uh, your valuable time, sir, so perhaps we may come down to business." Hemings nodded and put the bottle back down, then changed his mind and poured more of the whiskey into his own glass. Then he returned a bloodshot gaze to Callender, and waited.

"Our mutual, uh, friend tells me that you have some information concerning our newly inaugurated president. Some information concerning his relationship with your, uh, sister, I believe. With Sally Hemings." Callender leaned forward, a wolfish look on his lean face. "Is it true, sir? Can you confirm...improprieties? As was previously communicated to you, I believe, I can make it worth your while to share information with me."

Unexpectedly, a laugh broke out of Hemings, high pitched and hysterical at first, then degenerating into a bitter chuckle. "My sister, sir? You want to know about Master Tom and my sister?" Callender, taken aback by Hemings's outburst, leaned forward again and nodded eagerly.

Hemings slumped a little, then took a gulp of the whiskey. He looked back at Callender, assessing and weighing what he could read in his face. Then he seemed to gather energy and focus, seemed to have made a decision. He sipped the whiskey again, then leaned forward toward Callender. "So far as I know, Master Tom never touched Sally Hemings." Callender sat back as if slapped in the face, a look of puzzlement on his features. Hemings spoke again: "You want to know about Master Tom and Sally and...us? Let me tell you about it," he said, refilling his glass. He looked into the middle distance as he began his story, and it did not take long before Callender had paper and pencil out of his valise to take notes as quickly as he could.

....

It was September of 1783, and the tall, red-haired man sat in his chair by the window, looking out at a grey world distorted by the imperfect glass as much as by the rain that came down in sheets. He sipped tea from his cup, barely registering the opening and closing of his dressing room door.

"Master Tom, about your clothes today, sir," said the eighteen year old youth who had entered. "It was a year ago yesterday, as you know, sir. How about a change? You can put black aside now, here's your nice brown suit. Hasn't been worn in a year. Mistress, she always liked that one. Here, feel what a nice hand it has." He ran thin, light brown fingers over the nap of the fabric, offering it tentatively to the man in the chair.

Thomas Jefferson glanced at the suit, then up at James Hemings, smiled and shook his head. "Black will do a while longer, James," he said, and sighed heavily. "A year seems like such a short time. I will always miss her, James," he said. He looked back up at the youth dressed in the Monticello livery who stood beside him: thin, slight, with short curly black hair, bee-stung lips, and skin of a light coffee wash. Undeniably male, but a girlish and willowy curve of the body, curl of the hair, and maybe—manner? The boy looked as if he might be eighteen or even younger. "But, James," he said, putting out his hand and laying it on the youth's arm, "it was kind of you to think of it. However, just black today." The youth nodded but remained standing there, the freckled hand still on his forearm. Jefferson looked at his hand, too, as it lay on the livery cloth, and then removed it, sighing again. The feeling of warmth through the cloth, the evidence of another living creature... Thomas Jefferson decided that what he missed the most was the small things, the presence of touch. Oh, he embraced his daughters in a fatherly way, but not often enough. Just... just the contact of skin, hand on hand...or on arm. His glance flickered at James, who was now preparing a black suit for the day. Then he looked back out the window, yearning for something that he could not quite name, or allow himself to name.

The rain fell harder and harder throughout the day. Jefferson's correspondence and studies occupied him for most of the day, but boredom crept up on him in the afternoon as the approaching twilight seemed hastened by the gloom of the autumn downpour. Stepping outside to take some air, he decided to walk the short distance on a covered walk to the detached kitchen. There, amid Mother Hannah—

very round and very black in her white cook's uniform—and two of the serving maids, he found James, an apron around his middle and his sleeves rolled up as he wrestled with a lump of white dough. Jefferson walked over, poked the lump, broke off a piece and tasted it. "Brioche?" he asked, cocking an eye at James.

The youth's thin, handsome face crinkled into a smile and he nodded. "I am trying, Master Tom, but French cooking is so difficult when one hasn't really been trained."

"Hmmmppph" rumbled Mother Hannah, "foreign notions. Why, master, don't we have good enough food here in Virginia?"

Jefferson smiled. "We do, Mother Hannah, but French food is another matter entirely. Now, James," he said, "show me what you are doing here."

So often we come to crossroads, to ways diverging. Was this when it happened? There were so many casual touches, so many occasions… it was hard to tell. James took a fresh bowl and a new collection of ingredients and showed his master how to make this strange, new dough. Interested…in more than one way?… Jefferson stirred the dough, touched it, touched the butter, touched… touched his slave. Was this the moment when brioche became irrelevant, when some new revelation crept over the white man as his light brown slave showed him how to make French pastry? Surely, at the start, the white master shrugged it off. It was unnatural. He could not mean it. Yet… it had been so long. When did Thomas Jefferson look sideways at the beautiful youth beside him more than he looked at the dough? When did an unaccustomed stirring rise in his loins as the youth eagerly explained the process? Was it this time, or later, or some other lonely afternoon or evening?

Sally Hemings? Oh, she came and went on the fringes of his consciousness. She spent most of her time with Jefferson's daughter. Did she remind her master of his deceased wife? No, nor was he looking for such a thing. Consumed with his grief, he paid her very little attention.

It might have been another stormy night, but it was not. It was a warm summer evening. It might have been any evening; why that one? Why that moment? These things are unanswerable. James, in just a shirt and breeches, came to serve his master as he prepared for bed. Off came the white man's boots, then the shirt. Then Thomas Jefferson stood and the young slave knelt and slipped off the white man's trousers and... and the man extended his hand. Cupped the back of the youth's head, the soft, short curls. Let his fingers linger there, tentatively entwining in the thick hair. The white man felt the young man's head shudder. From fear or disgust? No... the youth held very still, his head down, still on his knees. His breath came a little faster, his thin chest rising and falling beneath the white shirt, his beating heart almost moving the fabric from beneath.

They stayed like that for a long minute. Then softly, once, the slave youth breathed the word, "Master." He brought a slim, tan hand up and placed it on his master's undergarment, just to the side of the center of the groin. And then he looked up. The tall white man looked into the youth's dark eyes and saw there—inevitability? surrender? love? At any rate he nodded and with his own hands tugged down on the garment a bit. Quickly, as if he had practiced doing so in his imagination, both the young slave's hands grasped the cloth and pulled it down, where it bunched around his master's ankles. The long, slim penis sprang out, growing quickly to full erection from out of a bush of dark red pubic hair. Thomas Jefferson gasped, stunned at the turn the course of events had taken, helpless to ask, powerless to tell.

Quickly but gently, James Hemings wrapped his slim brown hand around the reddening white penis and began stroking it. The white man gasped again and stifled a cry. Three strokes, and the youth's full, bee-stung lips encircled the man's penis and sucked it into his warm mouth. Shaking his head in a frenzy, the white man's legs began shaking. Both hands grasped the youth's head through the thick, short curls. Unable to breath, the white man mouthed "O! O! O!" and then the torrent came, almost by surprise. A year of abstinence, of dreams denied and thoughts turned away, came to an end. Groaning deep in his gut, the white man bucked out long ropes of semen, hungrily swallowed by the slave youth who still knelt before him.

The ecstasy passed. The white man, his eyes closed, still clutched the head of the youth who gently, thoroughly sucked the penis clean. The master opened his eyes and pulled his penis out of the mouth that surrendered it. The man looked aside, still clutching the youth's head. James Hemings, breathless himself now, waited on his knees, his gaze unavoidably fixed on the long, wilting organ before him. His master found a croaking voice.

"Thank—thank you, James," he said. He removed his hands from the slave's curly head, hands that fluttered uselessly for a moment. His head was still turned to one side, his gaze averted from the slave kneeling before him. "I—I will retire now. I do not need your help any longer. You may go to your bed."

"Yes, master," whispered the youth who rose, clutching quickly at the discarded clothing, mindful to perform his duties even as he was being dismissed. His own thoughts he had to keep to himself. Was he grateful that he had done what was wanted? Was he fearful that the master might regret that moment? Was he happy for the realization of something he may not even have admitted to himself before this? Perhaps all those things. The slave youth gathered the master's clothing and quickly scurried into the dressing room next to Thomas Jefferson's bed chamber where he would hang the clothing up—the dressing room where the slave himself slept on his cot at night to be near should the master call. "Good night, then, master," he whispered, and slipped from the room.

Thomas Jefferson's mind was a perfect tumble of thoughts and emotions. He could not reply, could not look at his slave yet. He stood there for another moment, and then decided to surrender his inner turmoil to the night. Without bothering to put on the dressing gown that lay on a nearby chair, the man slipped into his bed and extinguished the candle that stood on a nearby table.

In sleep comes clarity. In the middle of the night, Thomas Jefferson awoke with a raging erection. Decided, he threw the bedclothes back and sat up at the side of the bed. He lit the candle. "James!" he called. The youth must have been waiting, unable to sleep, for he immediately appeared at the door of the dressing room clad in a simple, rough, long nightshirt. "Master?" he asked in a soft, reedy voice.

"Come here," said the white man. James stepped up to the side of the bed. Thomas Jefferson looked him in the eyes once, then looked at the nightshirt and tugged at it. "Remove this," he ordered. James quickly pulled it off over his head. He wore nothing else. His own penis, not as long as his master's but thicker, was beginning to rise, its medium brown color darkening as it arced its way up and out of a sparse patch of tight, black peppercorn curls. Thomas Jefferson looked the slave youth up and down, then once in the eyes again. "Turn around," he said, "slowly." James Hemings did so, and the white man looked and appraised, his eyes taking in the willowy slim body, lean but not overly muscular, the body of a house slave rather than a field hand. The buttocks were rounded and firm, flat sided. The slave youth turned slowly, eyes downcast but watchful for a signal from his master.

Thomas Jefferson pushed himself back into bed and against the wall on the far side, and patted the space on the sheets between him and James. "Come," he said. With a sigh and a shy smile, the youth lay down and was gathered into the arms of the white man. Jefferson rolled on top of him and began humping him slowly, grasping his shoulders, his buttocks. Tentatively, then more assuredly as he was not refused, James pulled into his own brown body the white man who writhed above him. Then their positions were reversed and the slave youth squatted astride the man who lay flat on the bed. A white hand grasped the youth's thick, brown penis. "O! master, thank you!" the youth breathed as the hand slid up and down. One white hand ran up and down the slim abdomen and chest while the other hand moved faster over the iron cock. It did not take long before the black youth cried out, his thighs stiffening, his hips pushing forward, and two heavy gouts of semen shot out onto the white man's belly and chest. As soon as they did, the white man stopped pumping. "Clean it up," he commanded, and the youth leapt off the bed to find a rag to do so, still heaving with ragged breath himself.

The white man's abdomen and chest was dabbed clean, the rag put aside. Once more Thomas Jefferson reached up to his slave youth and pulled him into the bed again. Covering the brown body once more, he slid his stiff rod between the slim thighs and began pounding his hips up and down, his fingers around the youth's rounded shoulders as if to save himself from drowning, his head to one side. Quickly it came, the tingling in the thighs and lower belly, then the eruption as he slammed forward into the slave's body, filling the space between his tightly closed thighs with semen. The white men held that position as he recovered breath, then he slumped. The slave youth held him, whispering out a crooning sound. The master drifted off to sleep, still covering the black youth, who soon followed him into slumber. And that is how they spent that first night.

So it began. To others at Monticello, or in places they would visit, their relationship was nothing other than the proper one of master and slave. James continued to learn to cook. Master Thomas Jefferson continued to manage the weighty affairs of his household, and to participate in the affairs of the newly forming republic. They were careful—so very careful!—in public, keeping close custody of their eyes, being careful not to touch any more than was necessary. But how often at a formal dinner around the long table did their eyes meet in a flash, for but an instant, as James helped the company to a dish, clothed in his splendid livery. How often did they find themselves alone in the house, or fields, or one of the farm's buildings, and held a gaze for a moment before breaking it off, unwilling to risk what an accidental observer might see.

And yet at night—both of them novices in the ways of their love, they learned together, teaching each other, experimenting. And always, Jefferson was the master. Always, he directed their couplings. Always, he made his slave to turn slowly, naked by candlelight, to admire the slim planes of his body, the soft glow of his oiled, light brown skin. Always, he achieved his own ecstasy last, or sometimes he was the only one to do so, slumping into sleep over the willing brown body in the night. Always, except for the nights when he was tired or ill, and did not call James to him—and then James waited, listening, ready, far into the night.

The next year Thomas Jefferson was named envoy to the fledgling republic's most important ally, France. Of course, he took James, now nineteen. Jefferson told the world that the young man was going so as to learn better how to cook the French dishes that Jefferson loved, and no story could be more plausible. It was also true, Jefferson would put the young man to work learning to be a chef during the day, while at night the white man still summoned the brown youth to his bed where they struggled in passion far into the night.

They had not been long in this arrangement before Thomas Jefferson, always alert to his public image, began to wonder whether some of the French servants who came in and out of their world were beginning to—well, to whisper. Jefferson had another two or three slaves with him, but also some hired French servants. It would be impossible not to notice the closeness of master and servant. People in Virginia would see it as the natural result of having a valet, a close body servant, but would the French see it so? Were those looks of interest or speculation he saw, did he interrupt whispered conversations as he turned into hallways of his own house? So was hatched the "Sally" ruse.

Jefferson sent for Sally Hemings to attend his daughter, who was also with him in Paris. The young woman, child really, arrived soon and was established as his daughter's servant. Jefferson saw to it that he would be observed to flirt with the young, coffee and cream colored slave. He made a point of going into the same room with her alone and shutting the door, when that might be observed by French visitors and servants. He also did nothing at all to discourage the calls that Sally received from young French male servants of neighboring establishments. So when, in the natural course of things, Sally became pregnant, he likewise did nothing to discourage speculation that he was the father of the little one. Sally Hemings gave people something to gossip about, and diverted attention entirely from James—whether there had ever truly been such attention, or it was all in his imagination, would be difficult to say.

And all this time, James Hemings—when his master called softly to him in the night, he was always quick to go. Although the white man always brought the brown youth to orgasm first, he never lost interest or grew impatient for his master to finish. As his master's body clenched and pushed forward into his upturned, pushed-back buttocks, the slave's slim legs would curve back, his ankles hooking over the white man's to hold him there connected to his body a little longer. And so months passed, and passed into years.

But during the day, and the evenings when Master Tom was away at receptions and grand dinners, James Hemings perfected his craft of cooking. He studied with French chefs in Paris, and as he did so he saw how they lived. He saw how they accepted him as a fellow creature. James saw other people of African descent in the streets of Paris, free and freely going about their business. He knew soon after his arrival that slavery was not legal in France and that he was legally free. And he began to feel what that freedom meant deep inside of him.

The night came when James lay on his back, his arms and legs crossed over his master's back as the white man lay above him, filling his anus with the long strokes of his hard, red cock. James's own penis had grown rigid again after his ejaculation a few minutes before, and leaked a clear liquid that lubricated the white and brown skins as they slid against each other. Harder and faster the white man moved in and out of his black slave's bottom and then, stifling a cry, pushed forward hard, his body clenching, his fingers digging into the brown flesh of the youth's shoulders. The white man lay there shuddering, and then relaxed. James felt perfectly at peace, and although a slave, he felt a kind of claim over the man who lay upon him panting, his long penis still inside of him.

"Master," he whispered. "Ummmm," moaned Jefferson, his head resting on the youth's brown, rounded shoulder.

"Master, I love you."

A moment passed and again the white man grunted, "Umph," in a note of acknowledgement, and continued lying still.

"Master, I'm learning to cook really well. When we go back to Virginia, I can be your cook. I can prepare all your favorite dishes. I—I can make you happy, master." A single nod of the head that still lay on his shoulder.

"Master—master, I hear there is no slavery here. I hear I am free here. Master, I could be free back in Virginia if you wanted. We could love—we might—we could do this and it wouldn't be because I had to. Master—can I be free?"

There was a moment of perfect stillness, and then the white man pushed himself up off of his slave's body to look into his dark eyes. His wilting penis slid out of the loose anus as he did so.

"Free? Free! Boy, what's gotten into your head? What would you do if you were free? Put these silly thoughts aside." And the white man pushed himself off to the side of the brown body, then gave his slave a shove. "Go bring water and towels so I can clean up. And—and change these sheets while you are at it."

James fled from the bed to do his master's bidding. But a snake had entered the garden of his mind. A little place of uncertainty, of anxiety, had been prepared in his soul, and it would grow over time. Two feelings on separate tracks grew stronger and stronger, two juggernauts heading toward the same vanishing point on the horizon: James breathed the air of freedom in France and it entered into his bones. But he also sought the gaze of his master more, planned his steps to take him near to the white man, found occasion to talk to Master Tom more often. Holding the shuddering white body in his arms at night, he never felt more love—and he never felt more desire to love him as a free man.

James broached the subject of freedom—and of love—again, and then again. Jefferson was dismissive each time, and seemed to become a little testier with each dismissal. The soft whispers of love continued to be acknowledged by a muffled grunt, and then—by silence. As the white man seemed to grow a little more distant, James became a little more insistent. Love and a desire for freedom each grew stronger, two vines in a small plot of soil that might not be able to support them both. The two themes were rarely absent from James's thoughts. He decided to take more formal action.

The slave came to his master's side a little earlier than usual in the evening, as the white man sat at a small desk in his bedroom, writing. "Master, may I speak to you?" he asked softly.

"Well, James, what is the matter?"

"Master…I need to be free, master. I need that, sir. I am free in France, and I want to be free in Virginia. You…you wouldn't need to pay me wages back home, sir. I could…I could live with you. I love you, master, you know that, we…we could love each other better once I am free."

The white man sat still for a moment, then slapped the pen down on the desk. He rose and turned to James, as the slave youth stepped back.

"Enough of your importuning! You want your freedom, you shall have it. But you are my slave, sir, and I have invested much money in you and in your training here. I shall require that you continue to serve me for five more years after our return, during which time you shall cook and you shall train other servants to cook in the French manner. Then you may go your way."

James was speechless for a moment. Somehow it seemed as if it had gone wrong. "Master, thank you...yes, I will teach others, but only five years...Master, I don't want to leave then. I want to stay with you. Master, I—"

"Enough!" came a harsh growl. "You want your freedom, then take it, in five years. If you won't serve me, why should I feed you and clothe you?"

It came as a stab in the heart to James—and what followed, was it worse? In a quick move Jefferson stepped to the slave and slapped him on the cheek, then tore the youth's shirt off. "Remove your garments," he ordered, and undressed himself as James obeyed, trembling. The two standing naked together, Jefferson appraised the slim brown body of the youth through narrowed eyes for a moment, then shoved the youth roughly toward the nearby bed. James tripped and staggered onto the mattress, then made as if to lie on his back to receive his master. But the white man roughly grasped the youth's hips and positioned him on his hands and knees, his bottom facing the white man as he stood by the side of the bed. With a tremendous whack Thomas Jefferson brought his open palm down on the coffee and cream bottom of the slave before him, and then again and again as James stifled a cry of pain and surprise.

Stepping closer to the upraised bottom, now blushing a reddish brown, the white man positioned the slick and leaking head of his rampant cock at the wrinkled brown anus of his slave, and gave a mighty push. Lubricated only by its own slick sheen of clear fluid, the white man's stiff, long penis plunged entirely into the slave youth, who then did cry out in a voice that could not be stifled. "Silence" growled the white man as he pumped quickly back and forth, back and forth, and then with a tremendous push slammed his groin forward even as his hands pulled the youth's hips back toward him. He held that position, shuddering, then quickly withdrew from the slave's body. "Bring water and towels" he ordered. James, in pain, scrambled off the bed, his heart aching worse than his rectum, and went to do his master's bidding.

It was all downhill from there. There were other moments of sexual contact, other whispers of unanswered love from James to his white master, but they became fewer. A cold wall of separation mounted higher and higher around the white man, and the black youth could only lay an unsuccessful siege to that wall from outside. In another few months the Jefferson household packed up and boarded a ship to return to their homeland. James slept in a cramped corner of the steerage by himself all the way back.

....

James Thomson Callender's pencil stopped, poised over the filling roll of paper. Beads of sweat stood on his brow, and he held his breath. "And when you returned to Virginia?" he asked.

The thin brown hand reached yet again in the direction of the bottle, and missed. It slapped down on the table and slid toward the bottle, grasping it around the base, and dragged it near to the empty glass. It tipped and wavered, then the bottle upended. Some of the last of the whiskey went into the glass, some onto the table. James Hemings fought to focus on the bottle waving in his hand, then threw it against the wall. He turned his face to the white man, tears now streaming down the ruined, sunken cheeks from the dull, leaden eyes.

"He kept his word. I kept mine. I taught others of his...of his slaves to cook. Then he freed me, and bade me farewell and good luck. I found employment in a restaurant in Richmond and slept in a closet in the back of the shop—I was very lucky in that way—and sent letters to Master Tom, but he never answered any. I saw him in town sometimes. He saw me. He would nod and lift his hat. Nothing more. That was...a long time ago."

There was a moment of silence. The black man grasped the glass with both hands, bringing it to his lips, and drained it, then let it roll away across and off of the table.

"Two weeks ago he actually sent me a letter. Asked if I wanted...if I wanted to be his servant and cook for him in the city of Washington. If I wanted to be...to be his servant. To be his slave."

Another moment, and then great sobs began silently moving in the thin, ragged body of the black man, sitting alone on his side of the table. Between sobs, he choked out: "He...he wanted me but not as a free man. Not as a man. I loved him so, O! I loved him so, but I had to be free. I had..." And then, still sitting upright, the sobs took over.

Alarmed, unprepared for the raw emotion, Callender rose quickly, stuffing his papers into his valise. "I thank you, sir, for you help. I shall...I shall be sure to mention you in my story." He fumbled quickly in his pocket and threw a silver coin on the table. "For your trouble, sir."

James had no voice, only tears, only the shaking of his body. Callender gathered his things. "Well, sir...I must be off, sir," cried Callender, unsure whether he had offended with the silver coin, unsure what would happen next. The white man fled through the door. Reaching the ruined gate, he turned to listen, but the house held only an empty silence.

VIGNETTE

A black boy enters the shower in the bathroom of his home. It is the main place he can be assured of privacy from his parents and siblings. He is eighteen.

The glass stall fills with steam and clouds over as he stands under the warm spray. If he tilts his head forward the water lands on the short skullcap of tight, wiry hair, crisp as Velcro, a gentle sweet sandpaper of jet black, sharply trimmed to a distinct line from his neck to his forehead. He tilts his head back and the water sprays his face: the thick smudges of black eyebrow, the long, curling eyelashes over the almond eyelids, now closed and covering the hazel eyes beneath. His nose is broad but not flared, rounded around the nostrils. From just below the nose the flesh of his mouth pushes out at an angle to end in a wide top lip that flares like two flags, like the wings of an angel, purple or maroon mixed with brown. His lower lip is a full plum roll of similar color. The lips part for a moment, revealing a flash of perfect white teeth behind.

The water runs over a round chin and strong jaw, then down the strong, long column of his neck. Underneath his firm, round chin are a few whispy black hairs that he is too proud to shave. The boy's skin is a tobacco brown, deep and rich, a brown your eyes can get lost in. The water spreads out onto strong shoulders, prominent collarbones beneath triangles of muscle that run up to his neck. Over the end of each shoulder a wave of muscle rolls at the top of each arm, then narrows, then swells again in muscles above and below, more waves that rise and fall down the length of his arm. There are gentle valleys beneath the muscles on top and on the bottom of each arm, valleys where the beat of the boy's heart can be found in deep arteries. His lower arms are thin but corded hard with muscles, small branches of oak. The boy lifts first one arm and then another, rubbing soap into the short thatch of dense, black hair in each armpit, the white froth of the soap nestling into the thick texture of the hair. When he puts each arm down, you can still glimpse small tufts of hair sticking out.

The boy's rich tobacco color is darker where the skin is folded or creased, darker in the crook of his elbow when he bends his arm, darker in the whorls of the outside of his elbow when he straightens his arm, lighter in the lines of his light tan palms, darker along the neck when he puts his head first on one side and then on the other to let the water play on his small ears. His dark tobacco color is dappled with old, deep honey here and fudge there, and his colors shift with his movements as the blood moves from one muscle to another and as the light plays on the water rolling on his skin. Large triangles of muscle run from each shoulder down into his chest, the muscles pushing up the tight skin, gripping the bones of the chest hard in the very middle. His pecs are an inch and a half thick, each one, and just above the lower edges of their curves, a little to the outside, ride his nipples, very dark cones of flesh, not flush with his chest but tiny cones awash in the rivers of water that run around each one. There is no hair on his chest or belly. The boy stands by habit with his chest out and shoulders back, with his pelvis pushed forward in offering or threat, and his body makes a gentle "S" curve as he stands. The boy's dark hand slides over his chest with a bar of soap, then down the gentle valley between two rows of belly muscles, barely formed, just beginning to cover the soft rounded curve of a boy's belly that he is growing out of. The soap slides over and around his navel, a tiny ring of flesh with a snail of paler tan nestled inside just flush with the taut skin of the belly.

The small hills and valleys of his belly even out as his abdomen rides between the downward pointing lines of his pelvis, his hip bones making two arrows that point towards his groin. Down everything points, down everything goes, the lower belly and the hip line are arrows and his dark hand with the soap slides down as well, down into a short, dense thatch of jet black hair, heavy with water now, flecked white with the soap. Then down some more the water flows, over a penis that is now half-erect, a beautiful fruit, purple black, an eggplant, narrow as it leaves his body, swelling to fit the palm, then narrow again toward the small flared cockhead, now peeking out tan and red from beneath the very dark skin, the extremely dark folded foreskin that the slowly growing penis is crawling out of like a butterfly from its cocoon. The boy's dark hand runs the soap casually over the dark, densely textured scrotum that hangs beneath his penis, a scrotum dusted with the tiniest black hairs, holding two egg-sized balls within, each heavy with young sperm and hormones.

The boy soaps his fingers well, then puts the soap on the shower ledge, turns, and reaches behind him. The water runs down his strong back, collects in the deep valley of the spine between smooth, strong muscles, emptying into the tight canyon between his ass cheeks. His buttocks are slab-sided but rounded behind, and pushing up, higher above by just a slight angle than they are below. He could almost, but cannot quite, rest the soap on the natural ledge of his own high, tight, rounded bottom. He slides his soapy fingers into the canyon, lingering to push gently into the tight, brown and maroon starfish of an anus. The boy doesn't bother with his legs, with the strong, dark brown waves of muscle that rise and fall from pelvis to knee, then again on the back of his calves to his ankles; these can take care of themselves as the water rushes down them. The light tan soles of his feet soak in the water at the base of the shower as he stands there under the warm spray. The black boy is beautiful in his African body, and what is African about him is what is beautiful.

The black boy is thinking of a white boy he saw in gym class that day, the same one he sees every day. He has figured it out so he knows just exactly when the white boy hits the shower, knows just when the white boy is back at his locker. If the black boy hurries at his locker after the shower, he can be dressed and waiting in the painted cinder block hallway of the gym in time to see the white boy at the other end of the shower, still dressing. They have looked at each other beneath hooded eyelashes, out of the corners of their eyes, making secret unacknowledged contact, making a private bubbled world in the midst of the laughing and shouting of the showers after gym class. But they never speak. They share no other classes. Each time, the white boy is gone when the bell rings, vanished down the hallway ahead of him as the black boy emerges from the locker room, looking left and right.

The black boy is thinking of that white boy now, and has grasped his wet and soapy penis with his hand, put his palm around the swelling middle of his penis that seems made for caressing, is slowly rubbing back and forth, now and then clenching his tight bottom muscles and pushing something in his imagination out through the hardening, lengthening penis as his hand slides up and down his shaft. He is thinking of the white boy taking notice of him, of the white boy looking, of the white boy touching, of the white boy's rose, pale lips surrounding the penis that is now rock hard and throbbing in the splashing rain. His hand moves faster and faster now, thinking of the white boy. He thinks he knows the white boy's name, and he whispers it now. The name is your name.

Ten blocks away, a white boy pulls the shower curtain shut in the bathroom of his home. It is his only privacy from his mother and brother in their small apartment. The white boy steps into the steaming water from the shower. His cornsilk hair, which floats down over his ears and just brushes his collar, his hair which when dry catches any slight breeze and stirs, that blonde cornsilk hair now darkens and mats down in the water that flows over and through it. The boy is eighteen.

Water flows over the white boy's forehead and through the thin lines of blonde eyebrow, over the almond shaped eyelids now closed over eyes the blue of a summer sky, the blue of clean, deep water. His nose is small but cute, a pert button of flesh sitting above the pale rose of his lips, a rosebud that parts in the middle into two perfect petals of rose to reveal perfect white teeth and a pink tongue that darts quickly out then in, tasting the shower water. The boy's rounded cheeks show just a dusting of freckles. His cheeks and chin are smooth and hairless, and his hair makes elfin points that hang in front of his ears where sideburns will some day grow.

Water runs over the white boy's thin neck. His body is muscular but thin. The collarbones stand out from smooth muscles that lie passively from his neck to his shoulders. Each shoulder has just enough flesh to keep it from being boney. The white boy's chest is only lightly padded with muscle, the thinnest pads to show the promise of a manhood only recently begun. His arms have long, thin muscles, strips of promised strength with just the gentlest swell to them. He is not short for his age, but he has outgrown his muscles recently, and in some ways looks like a tall little boy. On the lower curve of his thin chest pads, in the middle of each pad, is a small, dark rose button of a nipple, perfectly flush with his flesh.

The white boy's skin is like peaches in a dish of cream, darker light rose and peach washed by off-white cream. He is a darker rose where the skin creases and folds, in the armpits where only a few whisps of dark blonde hair grow, darker in the scuffed whorls of his elbows when he straightens his arms out, a little darker in the crook of his elbow when he folds his arms, but lighter in the pale parchment skin of his palms. When he does fold his arm, the gentle rise of his arm muscles pops up a little, little rolling hills of boyish strength.

The white boy has no hair on his chest or belly. The belly itself shows only the hint of muscular development, just little swellings that pop up mainly when he bends over. When standing ramrod straight as he does, the white boy's belly has a slight curve out, a gentle wave of muscle sheathed in pink and cream skin. His pelvis is barely visible, no rolls but just a thin, thin layer of baby fat still covering his hip bones and making that curve of a belly from chest to groin. His navel is small and recessed, just a wink of a dot in his perfect, curved belly.

The white boy has been shampooing his cornsilk blonde hair. He has no soap. He slides his hands, sudsy from the shampoo, over his body, over this thin chest, down the belly, then around in back. He turns to let the water run down the tight, flat, thinly corded muscles of his back, past the boney shoulder blades down the slim back to the slim, flat sided buttocks, each one firm but rounded below, each making a perfect "U" when seen from behind. The white boy slides his soapy fingers into the tight slit between his thin, nearly-white buttocks, sliding up and down, then probing gently into the pink and reddish whorl that is his anus, pushing in to the first knuckle, then out.

The white boy slides his soapy hands back around to the front. He spreads suds into the dark blonde, small patch of hair above his penis. His penis was slack when he entered the shower, but now it is getting stiff. Not large, not thick, but a little longer than the dicks of the other white boys of his age, his penis slowly cranes its way out from his body, now it is standing straight up, and if he flexes certain muscles and tendons in his body he can make it slap a little against the wet lower belly. Thin, it nevertheless has a wide, flared hood, now completely freed from the dusky foreskin that used to surround it, a dark pink head above a rapidly reddening shaft. Beneath this stiff rod two testicles like small eggs are pulled up tight in a hairless scrotum hung just below the shaft of his cock as it arches up and away from his body. The white boy's legs are thin but muscular, the same long, gentle swell and fall of muscles you can see in his arms is echoed in his slim, hard legs. Pink toes splash in the gathering water at the bottom of the shower. The boy has inherited a beauty from his English and German ancestors, he is beautiful in his slim pink and blonde body, his whiteness is beautiful in him.

The white boy is thinking about the black boy he sees in gym class, the black boy he thinks is maybe a grade higher than he is. The white boy sneaks looks at the black boy when he can, and is sometimes surprised, and then afraid, when he sees the black boy looking back at him. He is often afraid in gym class. The white boy leaves the class as fast as he can at the end of each period because he doesn't want to answer any questions, and, much as he would like to talk to the black boy, doesn't want him to be mean. But the white boy can dream, and he does. He dreams the black boy speaks to him in the shower, showers next to him, reaches out to touch him when the others are not looking. He dreams they meet in the shower after school is over, some impossible chance bringing them alone there, and that the black boy encircles him in his strong, brown arms, pushes his thin white body against the wet shower wall and braces his brown feet against the wet floor of the shower to push into his white body. He thinks all these things as he begins to slide his hand up and down the vertical shaft of his thin, hard penis, up and down, slowly and slowly pushing his hips back and forth, calling the name that he thinks the black boy is called by. That name is your name.

Across town, the black boy's fist and lower arm beat faster, faster, sliding up and down the swollen shaft of his thick black fruit. He whispers your name, more quickly now. The white boy's fist and arm move faster, up and down, now his hips are pistoning back and forth, and your name is a high pitched squeal of a whisper in his mouth. Ecstasy surprises the black boy, gathering from his thighs and loins, while joy wells up in the legs and pelvis of the white boy. Two plumes of semen, each colored just the same, arc out into the air. Each calls your name one last time. Each fist slows, then stops. Water swirls down the drain.

MISTLETOE FARM
A CAUTIONARY TALE

Chapter One: The Shopping Trip

"A small house, sir, a small house, but I think you will find it in good order," said Aaron Hardwick, turning the key in the lock. Six months ago the door would hardly have opened, and then only with the squealing of rusty iron.   Now it swung smoothly back, admitting the master workman and his employer. Hardwick stepped aside and with a look of pride ushered the young gentleman within. Simon Simmons took off his hat, his pale, cornsilk hair swirling out from beneath it. Simon stepped into his new house and took a deep breath, noting the smells of varnish and fresh paint mixed with old applewood. He nodded with approval as his gaze swept the entry way.

"It looks remarkable, sir," the twenty-five year old owner of the house said to Hardwick. "Lead the way please, show me all the renovations."

With a nod, Hardwick stepped inside and closed the door. They stood in a bright, clean entryway, with a simple staircase going up to the second floor on their right and doors ahead and on either side. "Shall we begin with the drawing room, sir?" he asked, and led the way to the left.

Eighteen months ago, Simmons was not sure he wanted the house. A younger son, his parents had died in an unfortunate carriage accident two years earlier, in 1838. His older brother had inherited most of the family land, near Charlottesville, Virginia. It was only proper, as the holdings would be kept intact for future generations. Simmons had been willed this house, not a plantation by any means but more of a large cottage, on one hundred acres a little west of Roanoke, in the Blue Ridge foothills. A modest endowment came with the property, enough to keep it up and to keep Simmons comfortable. It took about a year to settle the estate, and during that time Simmons made his first trip to Mistletoe Farm to inspect his inheritance. He was appalled.

For years the family had rented the property out to tenants who scratched a hard living from the pockets of tillable soil that lay among the trees and rock outcroppings of these foothills. Then the property stood empty for years more, without adequate care and upkeep. When Simon Simmons first saw it, he was inclined to burn it down. The roof was structurally sound, although in need of shingles. But broken windows admitted birds and bats, plaster hung down in curls from the ceiling or lay in piles on the floor. Sapling trees sprouted in the outbuildings. The fields were choked with weeds. Yet, as he wandered through the house and land, a feeling of connection and ownership grew upon him. The land and house and its outbuildings were his, and a place to call his own. Here he could give up his position as a clerk in Charlottesville and live as a gentleman. Simmons calculated the cost of repair and considered his resources and made the decision to repair the house and have the fields put in order, as much as was possible. His generous brother, Hammond, helped financially, perhaps glad to increase the independence of his brother. Aaron Hardwick, a contractor, came well recommended, so arrangements were made and the plan put in place.

Now as Simmons was led through the house, he congratulated himself on his decision. Every room was in perfect condition, although each retained a feel of age and history. Fresh paint or wallpaper covered new plaster and polished wood floors gleamed, punctuated here and there with new rugs. Each room was fully furnished, some with items from the Simmons family place, some with new purchases from Roanoke. Upstairs, four bedrooms surrounded a central landing, each with a spectacular view of the hills and forests of the surrounding countryside.

Pleased with his employer's approval, Hardwick led the way outside. A nearby well house included a wash room with a large tinned tub, suitable for clothes or people as the need arose. Outdoor privies and other structures such as smokehouses, a kitchen, and woodsheds were arranged around the main house. A barn stood near small fields newly cleared and ploughed, not large enough for crops but certainly adequate for vegetable gardens. A grove of fruit trees lay beyond the fields, and there were enclosed pens for livestock, when those should be acquired. Two horses roamed one enclosure, their presence explained by the large wooden wagon housed in the barn.

Three more structures remained to be inspected: the slave quarters. Simmons had given specific instructions that these should be made sound and comfortable. Unpainted, their wooden walls were nevertheless tight against wind, rain, and the snow that would come in the winter some six months hence. A small verandah ran along the front of each cabin. Inside were simple beds, furniture, and a fireplace in each for cooking and warmth. Rough wooden dressers held simple clothes, pine cabinets contained cooking instruments and eating utensils. The clean smell of new wood and varnish floated in the air. Simmons nodded his approval, and gave further thought to his plans.

Returning to the cottage, Simmons wrote a cheque for the funds due to Hardwick, shook his hand and congratulated him, and offered him a drink of whiskey. Hardwick politely declined on the grounds that the sun was setting and he had some miles to ride yet to reach his home.

Simmons saw him off, then took his own horse, which he had ridden to this appointment, to the barn, where he curried and fed him and then put him up for the night with the two cart horses, securing the barn door against predators. In the gathering twilight, Simmons walked back to the house where he lit some lanterns and helped himself to a simple dinner from the provisions he had caused to be delivered to the house. Enjoying the whiskey himself, he sat on the cottage's spacious verandah for a long time, listening to the gathering night sounds of insects and owls, and the cough of the deer that moved stealthily through the surrounding woods. Tired from the day's events eventually, he secured the doors and withdrew upstairs for the night, to sleep for the first time in his new home.

The first chorus of birds awoke him the next morning. He reflected that once he had acquired some livestock, it would likely be roosters that performed that task in the future. Arising, he ate a simple breakfast, visited the nearby outdoor privy and then bathed quickly in the cold well water of the wash room tub. Dressing in the sturdy clothes of a Virginia gentleman farmer, he pocketed a large wallet, hitched up his two horse team to the wagon, and set off down the winding path that led to the main road toward Roanoke.

The journey took the two hours he expected it would. He crossed small creeks, some so small they simply ran across the road rather than under a bridge. Birds sang in the strengthening sun. The road was good but, like all country roads, pitted, with branches here and there that required clearing. Arriving in the small but bustling town, he purchased supplies from several merchants: Salt pork, lard, oil, crackers, dried wheat and corn in heavy sacks, dried beans, molasses, flour, cornmeal, salt, sugar, cloth, seeds for planting, plus a musket and a shotgun with powder and ammunition. At another merchant's he arranged for the delivery of two milk cows, a sow with a brood of young, several hens and a rooster. He purchased more whiskey, and then went into a tavern for his midday meal of corn cakes, boiled beef and vegetables, and beer. Refreshed, he stepped out into the street and up into his wagon. Down one street he went and up another, and pulled up in front of his final destination. A sign over the door proclaimed the nature of the business: BULSTRODE'S MARKET, FINE NEGROES BOUGHT AND SOLD. Simmons sat for a moment on the seat of the wagon, his heart beating a little faster, his breath coming perhaps a little harder. He had been thinking about this business for months. Taking a final deep breath, he stepped down into the street, secured his horses to a rail, and walked into the building.

The place had an indefinable smell—was it uncleanness? perhaps despair? A man built like a brick building, and just as red, sat in a large entryway, writing at a high desk. He looked up quickly, a keen appraising glance in his bright eyes behind bushy brows. With surprising speed and grace for one so large, he skipped out from behind the desk and approached Simmons with his hand extended.

"Good afternoon to you, sir!" he cried. "My name is Bulstrode." No other name was offered. Simmons took his hand, noting the strength in it, the surety of command and control, and introduced himself. "And what may I show you today, sir?" inquired the slave merchant.

"I am newly come into some property a little west of here," said Simmons, "and I need servants." Bulstrode nodded, his eyes piercing Simmons with a calculating, appraising look. "I am thinking I would like three male servants and three female servants, sir," continued Simmons. "If you have... couples here already, or people already connected in some way, I should be happy to consider them. But six servants, sir, three male and three female."

Bulstrode looked at the ceiling for a moment, thinking. He snapped his fingers, thick as small branches. "I have it sir! For four of them at least, we do have one pair, a man and a woman newly mated...I can't say 'married,' can I?!" he said with a wink, "and then one brother and sister, still youths. But a third couple... I shall have to think, sir, let me think. But while I am thinking, let me show you the property I have, and you shall decide if they meet your needs!"

Bulstrode led the way down a narrow hallway and pushed open the barred wooden door of a room. A soft murmur of voices ceased abruptly as they entered. It was a large chamber with benches lining the walls. Sitting, standing, or stretched on the floor were dark skinned people of every description: One or two family groups, many single people, old and young, male and female. Some looked terrified, some unhappy, some carefully neutral. It was, obviously, not a joyous circumstance for any of them. They all wore simple, sometimes ragged, but clean homespun clothing. Perhaps forty dark faces looked sharply at the two white men who entered, then quickly away, but as Simmons entered the room he was aware of continued furtive surveillance under heavy, curled lashes.

Bulstrode stepped quickly to the end of one bench and stopped in front of a young man and woman who sat together on a bench, hands tightly clasped between them. "Stand up!" he ordered them, then turned to Simmons. "Two likely Negroes, each about twenty, perhaps twenty-one years old. Accustomed to skilled farm labor, although not field hands. Just acquired from an estate sale to the east of here. Would you care to examine them?"

"Examine..." at that interesting word, Simmons's heart skipped a beat. His eyes wandered over the two who stood before him, heads bowed. Their fingers were still intertwined, furtively. Simmons thoughts raced back to earlier....examinations.

Raised with slaves ever present in his parents' home, his earliest childhood friend was Brutus. Nearly his own age, very dark, with a hard, slim body, he and Brutus shared every waking moment from his earliest memories. As they entered puberty, they shared their bodies as well, equally, with clumsy, giggling first gropings and then breathless strokings and suckings. At eighteen, on a visit to his cousin James's plantation, Simon Simmons was taken by his cousin to the loft of a distant barn where James had arranged for four slave girls to meet them. Commanding the girls to disrobe, and to disrobe them, James and Simon "examined" each girl in detail, and as their curiosity and passion grew they gave way to every form of fondling and intercourse they had ever heard of in song or dirty joke, being sucked, fucking, and buggering until their bodies were grey with the hay dust plastered to their skin by the sweat of their and the girls' bodies.

From then on, there was no looking back for Simon. Reuniting with Brutus upon his return, Simon led the way to the slave cabins, where Brutus slipped in and issued his master's orders to the girls within. Again and again in hay barns or clearings in the woods the "examinations" were restaged and replayed, the white boy firmly in charge and his black slave boy eagerly following suit, sharing the fruits of his master's power, tasting these moments of equality founded upon their shared male passions.

As Simon passed through his teenage years and entered his twenties, he played the part of the Southern gallant at balls and social gatherings, but his interest in the white women of his set was strictly for show. He lived for those moments with brown and black bodies, shared with Brutus each time. In the course of time, Brutus took his own mate, but shared her with Simon whenever the white man came calling at their cabin. When Simon came into his inheritance and prepared to leave home, he shared one last romp with Brutus, which ended with just the two, the white man and his black friend and slave alone at dawn, arms entwined around each other. As he planned for his move to Mistletoe Farm, Simon thought and planned for the kind of domestic arrangements he wanted in that new home.

Simmons's attention shifted back to the two slaves in front of him. "Yes," he said slowly, "these might do. Let me see her first."

Bulstrode nodded curtly and took the woman by the arm, leading her away. Her hand kept its grasp with the man's for an instant, then let loose. The man did not raise his head, but Simon could see from the corner of his eye how the slave's gaze followed the woman intently, and how the man's fists clenched silently. Thinking, planning, Simon followed Bulstrode and the female slave. The merchant went through a door into a small room equipped with a rude cot covered with a tick mattress, a wooden table on which lay a number of cloth rags, and a chair. The floor was a little sticky.

"Knock on the door when you are done with your examination, sir, and take your time," he said, then with an air of professional detachment withdrew, shutting the door behind him.

She was a full-figured woman, not fat but with the ample curves of Africa much in evidence. She remained standing, head and eyes cast down. "What is your name?" asked Simmons.

"Aphrodite, massa. They calls me 'Dite, though," she replied softly, her voice full and reedy.

Simon stepped closer and raising his right hand, hooked two fingers under the top button of the simple sack dress the woman wore. "Remove this," he said. Dite paused a moment, seeming to assess the situation, then sighed very softly and undid the top three buttons. The dress was so loose, already nearly off one shoulder, that it slid to the floor. Simon likewise lifted his finger to the kerchief she wore around her head. "And this," he said. Reaching up, she pulled the covering off, revealing a bush of springy black hair about two inches long standing out from her head. Simon willed his breathing to remain measured as he took in her appearance. Her face was round, the nose broad but not overly large, with full, thick lips. Dite's skin was a deep chocolate brown, and flawless despite a life of work on the farm. Simon turned her shoulder slightly so he could see her back—good, no scars from the lash. She had full, pear-shaped breasts, firm but pendulant. Below them the smooth, dark skin of her belly followed a curve down to her groin area, where a dense triangle of black bushy hair separated her two strong thighs.

A familiar passion began to flood over Simon, welling up in him, taking control even as it bade him to take control. His eyes sank down, down into dark chocolate flesh, and he was lost. Simon reached out and lifted Dite's chin. Up came her face, her eyes flickering, now taking in the white man who was appraising her, now looking away. Simon's fingers brushed over her lips and then her cheek. The woman's dark eyes flickered again, this time with perhaps more interest. Now both of Simon's hands came out and rested on her neck, then her shoulders, cupping the strong muscles of the shoulders and upper arms, squeezing them, sliding down the silken sable skin of the arms. Her head fell again, but now her eyes look directly ahead at Simon's torso and her lips were parted. Looking intently at her face to see what might be read there, Simon's hands shifted quickly, gently to her breasts. He cupped them, feeling their weight and firmness. Now Dite sighed, and her glance flickered up to the white man's face, then down, but she spoke not a word. Simon's thumbs flicked the nipples, now hard purple-black cones. Then his hands run down over her belly and stopped, lingering in the dense thatch of her pubic hair.

Dite's glance shifted downward now to where Simon's trousers were visibly tenting out in front of him. His own breathing was becoming harder, and he realized he must do something if he were to carry out his plan for the afternoon. "Go to the bed and get on your hands and knees," he ordered. The woman did so. Simon walked up close and cupped each large, round buttock in his hands, marveling once again as he had so often at the ample spread of the African female buttocks. Between them winked the brown starfish hole of her anus, and the dark valley of her vagina below, now visibly moist. Was it his imagination or was the woman's own breath coming faster now? No time to speculate. Simon quickly undid his trousers and dropped them, then likewise his undergarments. His erect cock sprang out, dusky red and purple, the flared cockhead leaking precum. He pressed the head to the vagina opening and Dite gasped, looking half around. He held it there but a moment, then pushed in. The black slave woman gasped again, then moaned, and one hand came back to rest against Simon's thigh as if to control his penetration, but it was not a serious refusal, nor did it have any real effect. He was fully sheathed inside of her now and, grasping her hips with both hands, began pumping his hips back and forth as he stood behind her between her spread legs, the firm flesh of his lower belly smacking against the ample dark brown bottom in front of him. Was she—yes, there was no mistaking it, Dite was pushing back, shoving her broad, brown pillows back against his belly and dick. He increased his speed to a frenzy of short strokes. It did not take long. Some distant part of his brain was careful not to cry out, which might bring Bulstrode in. His orgasm gathered in his thighs and loins and then slammed out of him, his semen pouring into the slave woman's body before him. Twice and thrice he slammed forward into her, squeezing out his sperm into her. He held himself tight against her for a moment, then the crisis passed. He pulled out, trailing a thread of white semen. Walking to the table he grabbed one of the rags and cleaned himself.

"Dress yourself," he said in a hoarse whisper to the woman still crouched on the bed. Wordlessly, she stood up and put on her dress and kerchief again. Simon likewise had pulled his clothing back up. He paused for a moment, considering her as she stood still with her eyes down, then walked to the door and knocked loudly. In a moment Bulstrode opened the door. "The man, now," said Simmons.

Bulstrode nodded and led the woman away. Did her head half turn in Simon's direction as she was taken back to her place? Certainly she did not look at her mate, who studied her closely as Bulstrode took him by the arm and led him into the room.

"Take your time," Bulstrode said again, pushing the black slave forward, as he withdrew and shut the door behind him.

Simon's orgasm had steadied his nerves, but he was still riding a strong wave of sexual mastery. Walking up to the slave, he tugged at the simple, rough shirt he wore and said, "Remove this."

"Yassuh," whispered the man, and in one motion shrugged the shirt off and dropped it to the floor. Simon studied his face. The man's hair was about an inch long, worn in a shock of tangled wool standing out from his head. His neck was strong and corded, the head wide and oval on top of it, like the head of a dick. The man was as dark as Aphrodite had been, a rich deep chocolate color. His lips were likewise full, the lower one a little lighter as it curled out from his firm, wide mouth. Dark eyes looked out and downward as he awaited the white man's commands. Simon's gaze traveled down to two square chest muscles, thick as slabs of beef, with copper penny nipples set along the lower edges. A well developed line of muscles rippled on his abdomen.

"What are you called?" asked Simon, as he stepped behind the man.

"Pompey, massa, suh." Standing behind him now, Simon admired the deep ridge of the spine, a valley between two strong rolls of back muscles, a trough descending down into the firm, high butt so typical of African men. Simon tugged on the back of the man's rough trousers. "Remove these," he said. "Yassuh," replied the black, and down went his trousers. Simon walked up close now and grabbed both of the rounded, firm, high buttocks, one in each hand, kneading them. The slave gasped slightly, and began breathing ever so slightly more heavily.

"I am looking for a couple that can breed. Have you and Aphrodite had children?" he asked.

"Naw, suh, but we only been together three month, massa. We can do it, I know we can. Massa," he said, his voice becoming urgent, "Massa, please, take both of us. Doan split us up, massa," he said.

Simon walked around to the front. The man's dark skin shone lightly, muscles moving under sable skin with every breath. For such a muscular frame, with thick thigh muscles running down to knotted calves, the black man had a surprisingly ordinary penis. Not small, but not the huge size so many Africans sported. It stood at half mast now above two unusually large, dark purple black ballsacks, the whole in a nest of short, tightly curled pubic hair. Standing in front of the slave, Simon reached down and weighed the testicles, feeling their warmth and the wet potential within. He grasped the penis. It stiffened, engorged with blood, and grew some in length but more than that it increased in width. Simon began sliding his hand up and down the shaft, a dark purple, nearly black, darker than the man's skin color elsewhere. The slave's feet shifted a little farther apart, and his breathing really was becoming heavier now.

"You'll see, massa, I has lots of spunk, Dite and me, we be good breeders," said Pompey, now breathing harder as Simon's hand slid up and down the dark pole. It was so wide that Simon's fingers did not touch as they encircled the hot meat. It glistened with a steady stream of clear precum that pulsed out of the thick tip of the penis at every upward stroke. For long moments the two men stood, Pompey's hands working, opening and closing, hanging by his side, now thrusting his pelvis forward in rhythm with the white man's pumping hand.

"Aaaah! I is coming, massa, look out!" breathed the slave, and then with a huff and a grunt he thrust his pelvis forward and held it. A tremendous flow of semen came out of the shaft that Simon still pumped, now more slowly. The white man was thankful it did not shoot out far or his clothing would be covered, but he was amazed at the sheer amount that welled up out of the ponderous ballsacks of the black slave in front of him. Still it kept flowing as Pompey pushed, squeezed, and held his breath, and then the black man slumped, and began gulping for air. It was over. A sizable pool of white semen lay on the floor between them, and Simon's hand was coated with the stuff. "Dress yourself," Simon ordered as he wiped his hand on one of the rags from the table.

"Yassuh," breathed Pompey, and as he did so he whispered again, "Please massa, both of us... we be good breeders, massa, you is gonna see." Simon was lost in the power and lust of the moment. This man, so much stronger than he, was so totally in his control. And he knew that he had just given the black man pleasure, as Simon had given Brutus pleasure throughout his youth. He said not a word, but took Pompey by the arm and walked him to the door. A loud knock brought Bulstrode quickly. Simon followed the merchant and slave into the large room as Pompey was led back to the bench, the black man followed by curious eyes and by more than one knowing smirk as he returned to Dite's side.

Not looking at him, perhaps knowing, she smiled a bit and reached over to hold his hand in hers.

"Now, sir, another couple, very likely and especially in another year or two," Bulstrode said, leading his customer up the line a bit. "Stand up" he ordered to the two slaves he stood before. "About eighteen, sir, brother and sister, newly purchased from the Richmond area. Perhaps dangerous to breed as they are from the same litter, but you decide, sir, you decide," said Bulstrode.

Simmons beheld a boy and a girl of about the same age—they may have been twins. They were about five feet tall, with slim, taut musculature evident beneath their baggy clothing. Their rich caramel color betrayed a white or Arab ancestor in the past, someone who took advantage of a woman in the slave ships or the castles along the African coasts. The boy's hair was very short, a dusting of dense, tight black hair hugging his scalp. The girl's hair was black but a deeper cap of curls framing her face. They looked remarkable similar: oval faces, the girl with a boyish quality and the boy with a girl's fine bone structure and long, curling eyelashes. They had button noses, not overly large, and full, outcurling rosebud lips of a more reddish hue than the deep caramel skin.

"What is your name?" he asked the girl. "Rose" she replied, her eyes cast down. "And yours?" he asked the boy. The lad paused for a second and said, "Thorn." Then added, entreatingly, "I ain't lyin', massa, it really is." Rose glanced at her brother sideways and giggled. "Hush up, wench!" commanded Bulstrode. The girl froze and looked down, fear in her eyes.

"I will see them both at the same time," said Simmons, calculatingly. "Very well, sir," said Bulstrode, and led the way, one slave youngster in each hand, back into the room. Bulstrode left Simmons there with a nod, and closed the door.

The white man walked slowly around the two and came to stop behind the girl. "Have the two of you been sold in a market such as this before?"

he asked. They each whispered "No, massa." A tension seemed to be growing in the air. They knew something was coming, but not what, nor whether it would be pleasant or unpleasant. Simmons nodded. Standing behind Rose, he tugged at her dress. "Take this off," he said.

The girl turned halfway around and looked up at him in surprise. "All the way, massa?" she asked. Simmons nodded curtly. She gulped, took a deep breath, and appeared to consider for a moment. Then, no options occurring to her, she slowly unfastened her buttons, waited another second, and let the simple sack garment fall to the floor. She shivered and stood naked before a white man for the first time. Her brother, who had been regarding her in mixed curiosity and concern, now gasped, and his eyes flickered from his sister to the white man standing behind her. Thorn's lips parted as he caught his breath to see what would come next.

Simmons stepped up close to the girl, his trousers tenting out again now, his penis pushing through the cloth against Rose's back. Her body was slim but muscled, her hips already wide and her buttocks already plump. Simmons reached his arms around to her front, hands placed on her belly. It was slim, firm, and muscled, the deep caramel skin dappled with light, honey, and chocolate, as the belly curved from her chest to her groin where a tiny patch of wild curls could be seen. Looking down over the girl now, pulling her into himself, Simmons let his hands ride up her belly, to cover her breasts. These were small, the size of oranges, but pert and firm, with nipples unusually large for the tight mounds on which they sat. Rose gasped and looked down at the white hands that slid over her flesh, but did not attempt to escape. Her breathing came now more quickly, through parted lips.

A few feet away, Thorn didn't know which way to look. His gaze shifted rapidly from intense examination of his naked sister, to the floor, to quick hooded glances at the white man...who was looking intensely at him all this time.

"Thorn," he said, "come nearer." The boy did, hesitatingly. "Closer." The boy came gradually to within a foot of his sister, his head turned to the side now, looking down. "I am looking for a servant who will breed children. Not a field hand. Do you understand me?" Thorn nodded rapidly and whispered "Yassuh" between his parted rosebud lips—every slave understood the blessing that came with not being a field hand. "Are you able to breed yet, Thorn?"

The boy blushed a deep red underneath his caramel skin. "I has tried, massa—well, a few times. Mebbe I is, I dunno—" his voice trailed off. "But I is sure I can, massa, I sure is sure!" His reedy adolescent voiced cracked once.

"Take off your clothes, boy," said the white man. Thorn glanced at him searchingly. "Here, massa?" "Yes." Slowly, but with a sense of inevitability, Thorn slid off his rough shirt and then unfastened the single button holding his patched trousers up. Both garments fell to the floor and he stood naked, a foot away from his naked sister who was being fondled by the white man who might become their master.

Simon's breath came uncontrollably faster as he examined the shallow, circular pads of muscle on the boy's chest, the puffy nipples that, like his sister's, were a little large, the tight but only faintly rippled roll of the abdomen as it curved down to the small patch of black curls in the groin. A slim penis above pendulous testicles was at half mast, rising in spite of itself at the close presence of his sister's female body. Had these two played these games before, Simmons wondered. The boy's lips were still parted, his heart could be seen pulsing the caramel skin of his chest.

"Show me," said Simmons.

"Uh—what, massa?"

"Whether you can be a breeder. Can you make the white stuff that makes babies?" Thorn blushed again and nodded quickly. "Make it," ordered the white man, as his fingers massaged the slave girl's breasts, tweaking the large nipples.

Thorn tentatively grasped his penis with his hand. It sprang to life, no longer at half mast, reacting to the slightest stimulation. Still slim but now longer, it curved away from his body and up. Slowly, then more rapidly, the boy's fist pumped up and down as it encircled his own penis, now darkening with the inrush of blood, and he began breathing more heavily. Perceptibly, the dangling ballsacks began pulling up tighter. The slave boy's head, turned to the side, now swung to the front, to look down at his own organ, leaking precum, but also to look a foot away at his sister's naked body, at the white man's hands that now slid down over her belly to bury fingers in the patch of black curls below. Thorn could not tear his eyes away from this, and Simmons could not tear his eyes away from the site of the slave boy masturbating. Faster went the fist, it became a blur, and then with a strangled cry the boy threw back his head, thrust his hips forward, and slowed his pumping fist as his penis shot out one and then two dollops of semen that arced in the air to land on his sister's abdomen. Nothing even similar to the copious flow from Pompey, but it showed that his eighteen year old genitals were fully functional. The boy's fist slowed and then stopped, then fell from the organ, which remained arched upward and out, oozing fluid for a moment. The boy's breathing was ragged, the penis still quivering. Then it, too, began to fall.

Simmons reached down to smear the white fluid on the girl's caramel brown belly, meditatively. Then, stepping back, he ordered both the boy and the girl to clothe themselves again. They did so, exchanging quick, questioning glances with each other but avoiding any looks at the white man. When they were clothed, Simmons stepped to the door and knocked. Bulstrode opened, nodded, and beckoned the two eighteen year olds to follow him back to their benches. Simmons took a deep breath and then brought up the rear.

Thorn and Rose deposited on the bench, Bulstrode turned to Simmons. "I'm afraid we have no other such couples, previously connected sir," he said. "But of course," and here he gestured expansively to the whole room, "you might make your own couple."

Simmons nodded. "Very well... show me unattached youths of about eighteen. A male first, if you please." Very good, sir. Bulstrode walked to the end of the line and proceeded down its full length, ordering first this and then that young man to stand. Making the whole circuit, he had about a dozen youths standing quietly, eyes downcast. He looked at Simmons, who nodded, and began to make the circuit himself. He examined each young man, some large and strong enough to seem to be in their twenties, some so slight they might have been younger than Thorn. A few he lifted the heads of with his fingers under their chins to study their faces. He made the whole round, stopped, then walked decisively to one in the middle.

"This one," he said. "I will examine him now." Bulstrode nodded agreement and led the slave into the examination room. Once again, Simmons followed, and Bulstrode closed the door behind him as he entered.

Simmons walked up to the youth, who stood with head bowed. He was certainly no older than eighteen, if quite that. He was very dark, nearly a purple black. Simmons lifted up his chin to look into his face, as he had done in line. The youth's eyes shifted away so as not to stare at the white man. He had a rectangular face with full, heavy lips. His nose was broad but not flared. Unusually long eyelashes curled over eyes that were shining bright with irises of an inky black. It was a face both male and handsome and girlish and beautiful. Simmons ran the tip of his index finger along the lips, which parted slightly. Then Simmons reached for the buttons on the collar of the shirt, and unfastening them himself, he likewise lifted the shirt off of the boy, who raised his arms to help. Simmons himself tugged on the simple knot in the length of rope holding the youth's pants up, which gave way, causing the rough trousers to fall. He stood there naked before the white man.

Simmons walked slowly around him. His shape and posture was the beautiful S curve of the African body, shoulders held back, a padded, muscular chest with purple black nipples, a muscular, curved sheath of a torso ending in a groin that flowed back into prominent buttocks pushed up high. Passing behind the boy, Simmons noted the rounded but muscular countours of his bottom. Coming back around to the front, Simmons gasped at the sight: his penis really was long, perhaps not unusually so for an African but certainly beyond anything possessed by a European. Not as thick as Pompey's, it was nevertheless a formidable organ, with heavy nuts below it, and a tight tuft of densely matted pubic hair just above it. Not completely flaccid, the pendulous organ hung nearly halfway down his muscular thigh. Simon Simmons was completely lost in the flesh and blood fantasy standing before him.

"What is your name, and how did you work for your previous master?" asked Simmons.

"I is Toby, massa. I worked on the carts and wagons, with the horses, massa. I—I wasn't in the fields," he added, hopefullly. But it was unlikely that, as dark as he was, he would have been used in the house. Yet his skin was flawless, reflecting no killing work in tobacco or grain fields.

"Did you ever sire a youngster?"

"Mebbe," he said, ducking his head and looking at the floor. "It's hard to tell, sometimes, massa."

Simmons nodded. With his own experience among the slaves of his parents' plantation, he could but agree. "Can you breed, do you think?" he asked.

Toby looked up brightly at him, then quickly lowered his gaze again. "Oh! yes, massa, I's sure. I can sure give a girl a baby, massa!"

Simmons walked up to him and said, "Let's see." Then he pulled up the rude chair by the table to sit in it before the slave. His white hand reached out to grasp the huge penis before him. Toby gasped and half-staggered, then regained his footing. Simon held the ponderous organ in both hands, then began sliding them up and down the shaft. Immediately the purple black organ thickened. It was already so dark, as dark as Toby's skin, that it could not have darkened any more. The skin, stretched by the growing erection, took on a satin quality. The organ grew to its full length, and now it really might have reached to the boy's knee, but Simmons held it straight up as his hands slid up and down, more quickly now. Precum glistened as it oozed from the tip and slid down the shaft, but the rod was so long it never made it completely down the mighty rod. Toby held very still, only a rapid breathing betraying the growing storm in his loins. Faster and tighter flew the white man's hands around the fleshy pole.

Suddenly, he uttered "Massa!" shuddered mightily and his knees nearly buckled. A rope of semen shot straight up and landed a few inches to the side on the floor. Then followed a continuous ooze of semen as Simmons's hands slowed, kneading and massaging the engorged rod. The semen had so far to flow from the black man's balls that it took a while to milk all of it out. Toby stood, his eyes wide in astonishment, staring intently at the white hands wrapped around his most private part. When it appeared that no more white spunk could be coaxed out, Simmons stood and cleaned his hands on a rag. "Dress yourself," he commanded, and Toby obeyed.

"Toby," he said, "if you are to be a breeder you will need a mate. Shall we find you one out there? Just you and me?"

Toby's eyes grew large again, a smile broke out on his full lips, and he dared to look searchingly into the white man's face. "A—a gal, for me, massa?"

Simmons nodded. "A man needs a wench, doesn't he?" Toby actually giggled, and nodded his head in delight. This strange white man was offering to buy a woman to service him. Toby's delight was also not lessened by the fact that the same white man had just, undeniably, given him a great deal of pleasure. "Yassuh, please suh, I promise, Ise a good breeder," said the slave.

"Very well," said Simmons, "we will go back in there and you will pick out a likely wench." Toby was nearly quivering with his unexpected good luck. Simmons strode to the door and knocked.

"One more servant, please," he said to Bulstrode when the man appeared. "An unattached wench, about the same age as this boy," he said. Bulstrode thought a moment, nodded, and once more made the round of those sitting in the room as Toby and Simmons waited, watching. Again, about a dozen young women were told to stand, and Bulstrode gestured to them and bowed to Simmons when he was done.

Simmons and Toby walked the line again. Toby was so excited he might have chosen every one, but Simon bade him look at each one first. It took two rounds but finally Toby turned to the white man and whispered something. Simon nodded and whispered back. Then he turned to Bulstrode and pointed back to one figure. "Her," he said. Bulstrode nodded again and led the young woman to the room. As he was leaving he made as if to lead Toby back to the bench, but Simmons stopped them, saying, "The buck will remain here." Bulstrode nodded and closed the door.

Toby stood directly in front of the young woman, about six feet away, and looked at her intently. Simon walked around the two, slowly. "What is your name, gal?" he asked, "and how old are you?"

"I is Venus, massa. I is eighteen," she replied in a soft but full voice, resonant with the reedy timbres of Africa.

"What work did you do for your former master?"

"I cooks, massa, and sews, and works in a garden."

Simon nodded. He reached out and tugged at the kerchief around her head. "Remove this" he ordered. She pulled it off, revealing a short cap of thick, kinky, utterly black curls. Her skin was dark, not as dark as Toby's but the chocolate shade of Aphrodite's and Pompey's. She had a heart-shaped face, lips full and moist but not too large, pushing out of a fleshy mouth beneath a broad nose. Her eyes looked downward, or shot furtive glances at Toby, from beneath long, curled lashes. She did not look at the white man.

"And remove this," Simon ordered, tugging at the frayed sleeve of her rough gown. The woman paused, sighed, looked again at Toby, then tugged slowly, slowly at the cord holding the dress together, as if to delay the inevitable. It gave way suddenly, her hand reluctantly let loose of the cord, and the dress dropped to the ground.

Venus's chocolate dark skin had a light sheen of oil on it. Her body was muscular but on a small frame. Her breasts were firm and very large, oblong like papayas. Too taut to sway, they bobbed as she moved. They were assertive, fleshy arguments presenting themselves to anyone who might want to engage with them. Beneath these magnificent bosoms, her torso narrowed to a small waist, lightly muscled with a prominent navel displaying a lighter colored button of flesh just inside. Then her hips swelled out in prominent, rounded buttocks leading down into firm, muscular thighs and calves. Her body was made of the flowing curves of Africa, exaggerated just a bit but not too much so. A small, dense triangle of pubic hair covered her groin.

Simon resumed his slow circling of the two. The girl's dark body was a spell conjuring up his memories of many like her over the last few years, enchanting him into a siren world of dark, warm flesh. Then he reached over and gently hefted one of the girl's breasts. Venus gasped and then sighed, but it was clear she knew there was nothing she could do. Toby, watching with parted lips and increasingly heavy breath, gave a nearly inaudible moan.

"Toby, come feel of her bosoms," said the white man. "Will she do, do you think?" Toby started, seeming to come out of a trance, and took two steps forward. He grasped both breasts reverently as the white man relinquished them to him, and cupping them from below, gently weighed them.

"Yes, massa," he croaked, licking his lips. Simon could see that despite Toby's recent orgasm, his enormous organ had begun to strain against the front of the slave's trousers. The three held that pose for a few seconds, then Simon broke the spell.

"Very well. Venus, dress yourself." Toby stepped back, reluctantly, and the slave girl complied quickly. Going to the door, Simon knocked, which brought Bulstrode.

"I shall take the six Negroes I have examined, sir," he said.

Pleased with such a sale, Bulstrode grinned hugely and nodded, pumping Simon's hand in his iron grip. The slave dealer issued quick orders to the six to gather their few belongings together. Aphrodite and Pompey, Rose and Thorn, Venus and Toby stirred, bewilderment, fear, and hope in their faces and in the looks they exchanged with one another. Bulstrode led Simon Simmons down the hallway to his private office, where papers were drawn up and money exchanged. The deal was concluded with another handshake.

"Now, sir, you have a wagon, do you? Yes, very good, if you will prepare it for departure I will bring your servants out to you."

Stepping out into the late afternoon sun, Simon took a deep breath, shaking his head of the fog of passion and engrossment in which he had wandered ever since entering this place. He unhitched his horses and prepared them for departure. Out of the building, clutching pathetically small cloth parcels containing all their worldly possessions, stepped Simon's own new possessions, blinking in the sunlight. Simmons ordered them into the back of the wagon among the new provisions, except for Toby, whom he ordered to sit by him on the driver's bench, where there was just room for one. Fully loaded, the horses strained and pulled and the wagon began to move forward.

West into the setting sun they went, toward Mistletoe Farm, the wagon steady but creaking and sometimes swaying with its burden. The heat of the day was coming off the rough roads and as they moved the last insects and birds of the daytime world grew silent, to be replaced by the night travelers. Rustling in the undergrowth to either side of the path betrayed the movement of deer as the soon-to-be-rising moon called them out of their naps. And in the wagon itself, the wary and appraising glances of the enslaved Africans among themselves, the stares at the white man's back, the whispered negotiations and explanations among themselves, echoed the natural world's slow turn into night and the strategies of night's creatures.

Chapter Two: Toby and Venus

A full moon lit the landscape as two tired horses pulled a loaded wagon toward Mistletoe Farm. Over the last miles of dirt road, the wagon crossed perhaps a dozen smaller paths through the trees, and on some of these stood silent black people, passing to and fro among the neighboring farms. They took their hats off upon seeing the white man on the seat, and eyed with sharp appraisal the load of human cargo in the back. Eventually the wagon bumped and swayed up the drive to Mistletoe Farm and stopped in the yard. There was a murmur of yawning and stretching as the tired slaves in the back and on the front seat awoke. Simon Simmons pulled the reins to stop the horses, rose stiffly from the seat, and turned to address his new slaves.

"This is Mistletoe Farm, your new home. I am Simon Simmons, your new master. Simon Simmons," he repeated, and the six newly arrived blacks repeated the name to themselves under their breaths, to memorize it. "First things first: I will show you where you will live, then we must unpack the wagon and see to it and the horses. Wait here while I fetch lights."

Simon stepped to the verandah where he had already prepared lanterns and matches. He lit four lanterns, one of which remained on the verandah. The other three he carried down onto the lawn. The lanterns were handed out to the three females. "Follow me, all of you," he said as he led the way to the first slave cabin. "Aphrodite and Pompey, this will be yours. Go inside, there are more lanterns there and all the provisions you will need for the moment. Take but a few moments to arrange matters to your liking, then rejoin us by the wagon." The couple murmured their thanks, taking the lantern, and entered the cabin. As the rest of the group walked away they could hear soft exclamations of surprise from inside. To a couple recently homeless and in danger of being sold apart, the modest accommodations of the slave cabin must have seemed like a palace.

Leading the way to the next cabin, Simon handed a lantern to Thorn. "You and Rose will stay here," he said.

"By ourselves, massa?" the boy asked?

"Yes," replied their master. "There are two beds inside, including one large one. Arrange yourselves as you see fit, and then come back out to the wagon." The two youngsters nearly bounded into the cabin, pleased to be "playing grownup" with their very own house. Squeals of delight could be heard as they inspected the new, simple clothing, the foodstuffs, and other provisions.

A few more steps took them to the last of the three cabins. "Venus, you will stay here. Light a lantern inside and look about you, then return to the wagon." Toby looked questioningly at the white man and made as if to follow Venus into the cabin, while she stopped in the doorway, casting a hooded stare at Toby. "Tonight at least you will stay in the main house," said Simmons, and after a split second of hesitation Toby nodded and followed his master back to the cart. They coaxed the horses to pull the still-packed wagon into the barn, then Simmons bade Toby to unhitch and attend to the horses.

As Toby led the team away, the other five slaves arrived in the barn, holding up lanterns and looking in curiosity at this part of their new home. Simmons gave orders as to the disposition of the supplies. Some were to go to the slave cabins, and were hauled away with joy— certainly, the material lot of these people had turned out to be better than they had feared, better than it might have been. Some of the supplies were to go to the main house, or the separate kitchen, some were to remain in the barn or other outhouses. Many hands made light work, and soon all the purchases were in their proper places. Toby finished his work in feeding and currying the horses and he rejoined the group. The night had come on fully by now, the light of lanterns winked out of every slave cabin and from the verandah.

"Tomorrow there will be more work, but everyone should take their rest tonight. You will find your duties are not hard and that I am an easy master," said Simmons. "For now, there are provisions for cooking in each cabin. You must be dirty from the journey, you are welcome to bathe in the wash house as well. I will see you all in the morning."

The group murmured their thanks and bowed to Simmons. Some scurried off to their cabins. Pompey remained for an instant, regarding his master thoughtfully, then he also turned. Simmons nodded to Toby. "You will stay with me in the house at least for tonight, perhaps— perhaps for longer, we shall see. Your other duties," and here he nodded toward Venus's cabin, "will begin tomorrow."

"Yassuh!" said Toby with a wide grin on his face. After his journey, he would not mind what he imagined to be good slave quarters in the main house, and he could gather strength for his duties with Venus. "Come," said Simmons, "there is food in the house, let us eat and then wash up." He led the way back to the house, where he lit lanterns and fetched some of the remaining food from a cupboard. The two men washed their hands and faces in a basin, which Toby emptied out into the yard. Simon helped himself to some crackers, apples, and cheese, then bade his slave to do the same, and sat down at the dining room table. Toby hesitated. "You want me to serve you, massa?" he asked.

"No, just take food and sit," replied Simon. Still Toby hesitated, then helped himself to a full plate and made as if to withdraw to the verandah for his meal.

"No, sit here, just there," said Simon, pointing to a chair perpendicular to his own. Toby hesitated again.

"Massa, at the table with you? It ain't right," he whispered.

"Sit," said Simon. Toby did so, still hesitatingly, casting sidelong glances at the white man. But the sight and smell of the simple food overwhelmed him and he began to eat greedily. Halfway through the meal he finally became aware of it: Simon, munching slowly and deliberately, was looking intently, fixedly at the eighteen year old slave boy. Toby stopped in mid chew, casting swift sidelong glances at the white man. He did not dare to look at him directly.

"Can I do somethin' for you, massa? Anythin' wrong?" the youth asked.

Simon kept staring for an instant, then started as if awaking. And he really had been in another world: a world of deep, dark color, sinuous curves and muscle masses, full straining breasts and heavy, pendulant penises, full moist lips under generous, soft, broad noses. Sinking into his slave visually, he was taken back to the world he had become lost in on his parents' plantation, a world that took up so much of his thought and imagination. He swam quickly back up from the depths of dark brown thighs and buttocks, tight, crisp hair and curling lashes, and surfaced in the dimly lit dining room.

"No—no, nothing is the matter. Continue eating," he said. But for the rest of the meal, both master and slave continued to eye each other furtively, each occupied with his own thoughts.

The evening was full of the sounds of insects and night creatures as Simmons and Toby stepped out onto the verandah after eating. Lantern light disclosed Aphrodite and Venus standing outside of the wash house, talking. Each held a length of toweling in one hand and a new, simple dress in the other, taken from the spoils of their new dwellings and their accommodations. From the wash house emerged Rose, the glint of water in her dark curls visible in the lantern light, dressed in her own new clothing. She greeted the women, then hurried on her way to the cabin she shared with her brother. Venus slipped into the wash house to take her turn. A few yards away, Pompey and Thorn sat on the steps of the nearest cabin, waiting their own turns. Had Simon or Toby looked, they might have seen the whites of Pompey's eyes turn and hold steady in the direction of the verandah, studying and considering.

"We will sit here and wait our turns," said Simon, taking up a rocking chair. Toby murmured assent and sat on the top step, a little below his master. Simon took in the night air, watched the progress of his new slaves as they came and went through the wash house, and through it all intently studied the short, tight skullcap of dark kinky hair on Toby's head.

The women finished their washing and Pompey and Thorn went in— together, it seemed. Was the twenty year old slave taking the eighteen year old under his wing, or was it something else? The moon rose over the compound as Simon and Toby waited. And then a movement caught the white man's eye: there, just beyond the trees that lay at the edge of sight, the steady shifting of dark shapes. Staring intently, he suddenly realized they were people, and most likely black people. On the move, a small group of them in a procession behind the trees. No doubt a path lay there that connected the farms in the region, he thought, and these were slaves heading home or going off for a night's furlough from the labors. The group passed and then all was still. Thorn and Pompey emerged from the wash house in their own fresh, new clothing, beaming wide grins, and made off for their own cabins.

"Toby, go up the stairs and take out two towels from the linen closet on your right at the top of the stairs, then bring a lantern," Simon ordered. Toby ran into the house and took perhaps a minute longer than was necessary to return; Simon surmised that he had been stealing quick glances at the accommodations on the second floor. Toby followed Simon, carrying the towels and a lantern, to the wash house.

The tinned tub stood empty, a trickle of water coming out of the bung hole near the bottom. Simon plugged the hole again and ordered Toby to fill it half way with water from the nearby pump. It took but a moment, as the tub was not large. Simon began to undress.

"Can I help you, massa?" asked Toby. His master nodded agreement and began handing his clothing, dusty from the day's activity, to the slave. Off came boots, then outer garments, Toby carefully folding each item as it was handed to him. Simon kept his eyes on the slave's face as he removed each piece, watching him intently as he loosened and then removed his undergarment. Toby's head hung down, but Simon could see his eyes riveted on his own body: of average muscular build, about six feet tall, the development of an active, athletic gentleman but not a field worker, a small nest of blonde hair in the pyramid between his chest pads that trailed down to a soft bush of blonde-brown pubic hair. Simon saw, or thought he saw, or wanted to see, Toby's eyes linger on the ordinary sized pink and reddish penis hanging over two large testicles.

"Have you seen a white man naked before, Toby?" he asked.

The slave youth started, gulped and shook his head rapidly. "Nassuh, never. White boys when I was a boy an' we was swimmin' but no white men, massa."

Simon nodded, pleased with the information that he was a spectacle, a curiosity, perhaps even an attraction? to this black eighteen year old. He squatted in the tub and washed, while Toby stood by, a little behind him, and Simon felt sure that every inch of his own flesh was being scrutinized by the black teenager. Finished, he stood up and accepted the towel that Toby handed him. As he dried himself he instructed the slave to empty the tub and refill it for his own bath. It was quickly drained and then filled again, and Toby stood, uncertainly, by the side. Simon was drying off, very slowly, still.

"Go ahead, bathe," the white man instructed the slave. Toby nodded quickly, then shed his simple garments. His body was as graceful as it had seemed earlier that day when Simon had masturbated him at Bulstrode's market. Toby slid the S curve of his muscular body into the small tub and washed, the tip of his enormous penis floating back up to peek out of the water like a turtle surfacing. Still Simon dried himself, using the towel to hide his growing erection. Toby rose when he was finished and pulled the bung from the tub, then began to towel himself quickly.

"Massa, we ain't got no clean clothes. You wan' me go get you some?" he asked. It was a situation Simon had, of course, foreseen.

"No, we will wrap towels around ourselves and retire to the house. Leave our dirty clothes here, the women will wash them tomorrow." Toby nodded agreement and wrapped the towel around his waist, his ponderous organ creating a ridge in front. The two men walked out onto the lush grass, barefoot, stopping only at the outdoor privy to relieve themselves, first Simon and then Toby. Entering the house, they extinguished all the lanterns but one and then went upstairs, towels still their only coverings.

At the top of the stairs Simon turned left into his room. Toby hesitated on the landing. "Massa, where my room? You wants me to sleep on the floor?"

"No," said Simon, "not on the floor. You must get a good rest for your duties tomorrow." Here he smiled at Toby, who caught his meaning and grinned back hugely, thoughts of the luscious Venus in his head.

Simon continued: "But we have had no chance to prepare a pallet for you, for the floor. Sleep in my bed, it is commodious enough."

Again, Toby's eyes grew wide. "Naw, massa, it ain't right, to sleep in your bed."

"It will be alright, Toby. After tonight…. well, we shall see." Simon moved farther into the room, setting the lamp on a bedside table. Toby stepped hesitantly in, surveying the modest but comfortable room with the sturdy double bed. Simon walked to a window and pulled the curtains aside so as to look out onto the yard. The cabins now were dark, although he thought he could hear faint sounds coming from one of them. And there—once more, behind that line of trees, illuminated by a bright moon, moved two or three dark shapes. There must be a path there, he would have to investigate tomorrow. He turned from the window and moved toward the bed, pulling off his towel as he reached it and hanging it over the back of a nearby chair.

"Let us retire, Toby."

"But…massa, you don't wants me naked in the bed by you, does you?"

"Yes, of course," said Simon, who opened a chest and brought out a set of simple, clean clothes which he had placed there strategically, anticipating this moment even before he left for Roanoke. "Tomorrow you may dress in these," he said. Then Simon slipped under the top sheet himself and then, turning to the lamp, extinguished it. Moonlight replaced lamplight with a silver wash. "To bed, Toby," Simon said.

Toby hesitated a moment more, then removed his own towel and put it across the back of a chair. His dark form seemed like a distillation of the night as it moved through the moonlight, the sheen of his skin catching the gleams from the window. He slipped under the sheet and lay there quite still, but also quite close to his master, as the bed was large but not overly large for two grown male bodies.

The two lay on their backs side by side for a few moments. Then, Simon shifted onto his side to face Toby, as if settling in place for the night. The unaccustomed closeness of the white male body excited Toby with its newness, but he was fearful of what would happen and quite uncertain of how he should behave. He had certainly experienced physical intimacy with other boys while growing up, but as he had said, this closeness to a white man was totally new to him. And yet—he hardly knew what he hoped, or dared to think might happen. His hand, lying at his side next to his master, must have been very close to the white man's penis...

Casually, as if it were the most natural thing to do, Simon flung an arm across Toby's torso. Toby caught his breath and turned his head slightly, risking a glance at his master. Slowly, almost randomly at first, Simon began to glide his hand over the smooth, hairless dark skin. Small circles around the muscular pads of Toby's chest, then more intentionally circling the nipples, slow rolling of their tender tissue and gentle pinches as the tissue began to swell. Then slow spirals down onto the muscled belly, down farther, skirting the small dense patch of pubic hair. Simon could see in the moonlight that the sheet over the slave's large penis was beginning to rise. Toby gulped and lay very still. As the white man's fingers began running through his pubic hair, pressing against the top of his penis, he caught his breath, and then he could stand the uncertainty no longer. Toby whispered urgently, "Massa! What you want me to do?"

By way of answer, Simon threw back the sheets. Unbound, Toby's noble organ sprung up, but was too large to stick completely straight up in the air. Simon grasped it, causing his black teenage slave to gasp and moan slightly. Simon gently laid it back up along the youth's torso, where it reached almost to his chest. And then in one smooth motion, the white man rolled over on top of the black boy. His own penis, now slick with precum, found a natural cavern between the black's muscular thighs, just beneath his testicles, and the white man's rod slid down between the boy's legs. Simon himself slid downward even farther in a sense. He slid down into black and dark brown, down into the world of ownership of dark bodies. His hands slid over dense, crinkly hair while his lips and tongue nuzzled full, rolled, moist lips. Simon's hands cupped the ripe fruit of shoulder muscles and reached down and beneath to squeeze the globes of firm, rounded buttocks. Toby, utterly unsure of what to do that would not offend his master, unsure of what he himself wanted, at first lay helpless. Then, giving in to the moment, he began to caress the white man's back, daring to squeeze the white rump as it moved up and down, in and out, as the master fucked him between his thighs. Toby ran his fingers through the soft cornsilk hair of the white man who covered him. Faster and harder Simon pumped in and out, in and out, until with a mighty shove he came, thrusting downward, gasping, draining semen down onto the sheets and into the lower part of the boy's ass crack. Simon shivered and clenched Toby's shoulders tightly, pumped and squeezed, and then it was done. He slumped, and in his ecstasy and the exhaustion of the day, fell asleep almost immediately. Toby lay beneath him, his own penis painfully erect beneath the master's body, not sure of what to do. As the white man's breathing became heavier, Toby risked a slight turn, which caused the master's body to roll off and onto his back, his penis coming out from between the dark chocolate thighs with a slurping noise. Still Simon slept. Toby lay for a few minutes more, his erection demanding attention but yet he was unwilling to do anything that might bring censure from the master. Soon, his own tiredness overwhelmed him and he slept, side by side with the white man who had just taken pleasure with him.

Simon awoke in the morning light, memories of the previous day flooding back to him, of a piece with his dreams of dark and sensuous bodies. He sat up in bed and looked to his side. Toby was not there, a crusty patch of semen on the sheets the only visible sign that he had spent the night. Simon rose, still naked, and walked to the window to look out. Smoke from cooking fires curled lazily from the chimneys of each of the slave cabins. Looking to the wash house, he saw Toby standing just outside in his new clothing; evidently he had bathed this morning and donned his new finery. And Toby was talking to Venus, whose foot was on the threshhold of the wash house, evidently just going in. Simon could only hear a lilt of voices from where he stood, but it was clear from stance and gesture that Toby and Venus were playing out the age old game of pursuit and evasion—and capture. No doubt Toby had emphasized what was likely clear to her in the slave market, that he was to become her sexual partner. Well, it seemed to Simon as if she were not positively repulsed by the idea, for at least she continued her bantering with the young male for a few minutes before disappearing into the wash house.

Sponging himself at a basin filled with water, Simon walked downstairs to find that Toby had returned to the house and prepared another simple meal. "Mornin', massa," he said, his head down and eyes averted. What had passed between them the night before hung in the air like a question.

"Good morning, Toby," said Simon, who then walked up to his slave and put a hand on the back of his neck, squeezing it lightly. Toby grinned, assured that he was still in good graces with his master—and was he anticipating more of the same intimacies? He served his master breakfast and was once again asked to sit at the table to eat his own. The slave did so, more easily now than he had the previous evening.

Halfway through the meal, Simon broke the silence. "Toby," he said, "would you like to be my house servant? To attend to matters inside? The women can help with the cooking and laundering, of course. And of course, you would still work with the horses and so forth outside."

Toby's heart leapt. Not so much from a love of indoor work, as from the realization that every slave held of the privilege that came with being a house servant. Usually, extremely dark slaves such as Toby would not have been considered for such work, but his was not to wonder why. He enthusiastically replied, "Yes, massa," and then a thought occurred to him: "But, massa—Venus?"

"Her cabin is not far away," said Simon. "You can spend the nights there and return here in the morning, or spend the nights here and visit her during the day, as you wish. There is more new clothing for you in her cabin, as I am sure she has discovered by now."

Toby grinned and hung his head bashfully. "Yes, massa, she has. I done heard about it! Yes, massa, I be your house servant, thank you massa."

Simon nodded agreement, then bade Toby clear up the table and join him outside. In the morning sunlight, Simon called his new slaves together. They all looked rested from the night, a little more relaxed given their good physical accommodations in the cabins, but still a little wary as they gathered to learn their new tasks. Simon organized them according to their talents and strengths. The females were assigned to wash clothing and linens and to set up the outdoor kitchen for cooking food for the main house and for the slaves. The males were assigned to plant what kitchen crops might be planted yet in mid-summer in the newly cleared fields, and to prepare the barn and enclosures for the livestock that would arrive today.

Everyone began their tasks willingly, and Simon walked to and fro, here and there, directing and encouraging everybody. The pleasant smells of bread rising and preserved meats cooking wafted through the air from the kitchen. In late morning the creak of wagons could be heard coming up the drive, and soon the shipments of livestock and other supplies in large wagons from Roanoke could be seen coming up the way. All other work stopped as attention was paid to herding the new acquisitions into their appointed homes, while Simon tipped the drivers and wrote out standing orders for provisions to be delivered once a week. The drivers were given food and drink as well, and left in a jolly mood. The homely sounds of grunting and clucking could now be heard, and the place seemed more like the working farm that it was destined to be. After a brief break for a midday meal, work resumed.

The women joined the men in tending the small fields and planting new crops in the afternoon, their domestic arrangements complete. Toby made sure he worked near Venus, and a playful if guarded banter continued between them. As Simon stood between the orchard and the vegetable plots, he was aware of another small group of people moving in a line behind a wall of trees along another edge of the field. He called to Pompey and bade him run over to the group to find out who they were. Pompey quickly obeyed and caught up with them. After speaking with them for a moment, he ran back to his master.

"They is from White Springs, massa, about four miles yonder," he said. "They says they takes this path sometimes." Simon nodded. So it was true; Mistletoe Farm contained several paths used by the slaves of neighboring farms, a semi-secret network of connections keeping friends and family in touch with one another. He was sure this was true on the neighboring properties as well.

The afternoon turned into evening. The livestock were attended to, new rhythms of work being established and new responsibilities assigned to each slave. Everyone stopped for a simple evening meal, and then dispersed to rest. One by one, everybody, including Simon (attended by Toby), repaired to the wash house to clean off the soil of the day's work. Evening shadows lengthened as the slaves retired to their cabins, and Toby and Simon sat on the verandah.

Toby seemed increasingly restless. He shifted his gaze between his master in a rocking chair and the cabin where Venus's lantern shed a solitary gleam into the night. Simon was aware of it, but was biding his time. Finally, he spoke: "Toby, are you ready to visit Venus?" Toby leapt to his feet, giving a heartfelt assurance. Simon rose, leaving a lantern on the porch, and walked down the steps toward the cabin, beckoning his slave to follow.

"You comin' too, massa?" asked Toby. Simon merely nodded. At the cabin door, Simon knocked, then opened the door without waiting for permission. Venus had been sitting at the rough wooden table, sewing. She stood up, a guarded look on her face.

"Venus, you know Toby," Simon said. She nodded and whispered, "Yes, massa."

"You are to take him as your man for a while. I want the two of you to breed, bring up some strong children. Do you understand?" Venus stared hard at Toby, then gave a swift glance at her master and cast her eyes down. It was clear that her emotions were mixed. Toby was not unwelcome, but the nature of her situation was. After a moment she nodded and whispered, "Yes, massa."

"Very well," said Simon. He gestured toward the bed, wide enough for two, that stood in the corner. "Remove your clothing and lie there," he ordered. Turning to Toby he likewise commanded, "Remove your clothing." Both slaves began to comply, then paused and looked at the white man.

"Massa," said Toby, "you wants us to wait 'till you go?"

"I'm not going," he replied, "I want to make sure the deed is done well. I am staying." And with that he pulled up a chair to the side of the bed and sat, arms crossed. Venus and Toby looked at each other for a moment, then with a sense of resignation—and perhaps of interest?—continued undressing. Both were naked, and Toby's large penis was beginning to fill and rise in anticipation. Venus cast a doubtful eye on it, then walked to the bed and lay down on it, waiting.

Toby crossed to the bed and lay down beside her, on the side where Simon sat. He reach out his nearly black fingers and tentatively caressed the dark chocolate breasts, full and long like papayas. Venus gasped, then sighed. As the black youth's massaging and tweaking became more assertive she turned a little on her side toward him and began rubbing her hands over his smooth, muscled chest. With little shifts they drew closer, hands now gliding over sides and down thighs. Palms cupped heads, running over short, crisp kinks or through tight, dark curls. Full lips met full lips, and passion began to overcome whatever hesitancy Venus had felt. Their breathing became heavier, and small gasps and moans kept up a murmur of passion. Simon could see from where he sat that Toby's penis was now fully erect, ponderously large and craning out to rub against the dark chocolate skin of the slave girl's thighs. Simon began to rub his own straining cock through the cloth of his trousers, which were being pushed out in front. He could not tear his eyes away from the scene being played out in front of him, losing himself in the moving dark limbs and torsos that were now rolling and wrestling, lantern light shining on the soft sheen of sweat that was gathering on their skins.

Toby shifted positions now to lie on top of Venus. His large penis lay between them like a flagpole, and he slid up and down on her warm, dark belly, his organ squeezing out a little precum between her breasts. Then he drew back on his haunches between her legs. He parted them and placed the large meaty head of his purple black organ against her wet vagina. He gave a tentative push, and Venus cried out in protest and put her hands against his thigh and chest. Toby rocked back on his haunches again and slowly slid the leaking head of his mammoth cock up and down in the entrance to her vagina, lubricating it with the flow of precum, then pushed again. It was no better. Venus cried out again, "It's too big!" she exclaimed. Once more Toby tried lubricating the vagina entrance with his own juices, Venus shivering as the fleshy cockhead rubbed her clitoris, but the difficulty remained. At this point Simon stood up slowly, as if moving in a dream.

"She is still a little nervous, and needs to relax enough to receive you," he said. "She needs to be prepared." Toby was shivering with pent up desire and rocked back again on his haunches. "What we gonna do, mass?" he asked, breathlessly. By answer, Simon quickly tore off his own clothing, casting them on the floor around him, never removing his gaze from the dark bodies on the bed. "She needs to be—opened up, stretched gradually. I will do it," he said. Venus turned her head quickly to look at her naked master with wide eyes, realizing what was about to happen. She herself was so caught up in the moment, so given over to her own sexual passions, that she did not offer the resistance she might have had Simmons simply approached her directly and on her own. Simon took a step toward the bed.

"Lie on that side," he told Toby, and the black youth flopped over onto the far side of the bed, his glistening rod slapping against Venus's torso. Simon slipped onto the bed on his hands and knees and, bending over Venus, began to rub his white fingers over her body as Toby had done but moments before, hefting and massaging her full breasts and rubbing her rounded belly. Toby stared intently, first at the woman's body and then at the white man's. Venus gasped and sighed again and, after a minute, reached out to caress her master's pink and red penis, now rock hard and leaking precum. Simon moaned and allowed her ministrations for a moment, then slipped back to take up position between her legs himself. Placing his slick cockhead against her vagina he pushed slowly. He was not nearly Toby's size, and Venus had relaxed a little from the black man's earlier attempts. Simon entered her easily in one long push. Venus arched her back and cried out, not in pain so much as surprise and pleasure. Her heavy breasts wagged as she writhed in passion, and then they were pressed down as Simon lowered himself onto her. He clutched her muscular shoulders to pull himself into her, and began pumping back and forth, back and forth. His eyes open, he looked deep in the eyes of the black woman beneath him, nuzzled her fill lips with his, buried his face in her cap of dark curls, his hips pistoning faster and faster.

Toby lay close enough to touch both the white man and the black woman, his lips parted as he studied their every move. His penis strained up against both bodies, now slapping against Venus's chocolate flesh, now against the white and tan flank of the master as he pumped faster and harder into the slave girl. With his hands he caressed the black girl where she was not covered by white flesh, and he dared to put his hand on his master's buttocks, feeling them clench and relax rhythmically. The three held this position, then Simon gasped, swallowed hard, and cried out, pushing his penis hard into the black body beneath him, hands pulling himself down into her dark flesh. Venus wrapped her arms around his broad, white back and pulled her master down into herself. His cornsilk hair fell down over her face. Shivering and gasping, Simon held that position as his semen flow slowed to a trickle. Then he grew still, and finally pulled out of Venus with a plop and rolled off to lie beside her on the bed.

"Now," he said to Toby, who needed no more encouragement in his growing passion. Flipping over quickly to lie between the slave girl's legs, he positioned his engorged penis at the head of her vagina, which was already leaking the white man's semen, and pushed. It entered now, in a long but slow slide. Venus arched her back and cried out, this time with some discomfort. Toby paused, then resumed pushing, and she cried out again. But his passage was lubricated by the load of the master's semen that lined the slave girl's vagina, and before long he was fully landed inside of her. Slowly he began pumping back and forth, holding himself up off of her body with extended arms, looking down at her writhing flesh. Discomfort gave way to ecstasy as Venus moaned and thrashed, her entire body cavity feeling as if it were filled with the black boy's enormous penis.

Simon stared at the struggling dark chocolate bodies from inches away. Leaning in, he licked biceps and shoulders, gently bit ears, tasting the sweat that was pouring off the dark flesh. As Toby's rhythmic pumping increased in speed, Simon held his open palm above the firm balloon butt of the black man and slapped it as it rose on every upstroke. Then he reached his hand in between the two to caress Venus's breast. Soon she reached her own ecstasy, stimulated by the white and now the black man beyond endurance, and she cried out, her fingers scratching and tearing at the muscular shoulders and chest pads of the black youth who arched above him. The tightening of her vagina in her orgasm brought him over the edge as well. He bucked twice and slammed forward, groaning, his eyes shut tight, squirting out his load of semen into the slave girl to join the white man's spunk that was already there. Pushing and gasping, he held the position until his crisis past. Then, exhausted, he slumped down and onto the slave girl, his penis still firmly anchored within her. Simon threw his arm over the black youth's heaving back and pulled himself into their embrace.

The three slept like that for perhaps an hour. Simon awoke with a sense of being in a strange place. His two slaves still slept, Toby still on top of the girl, anchored by his huge organ that was still inside of her. Quietly, Simon slipped out of bed and dressed, the two on the bed not waking. The white man extinguished the lamp and then slipped out the door into the night. He made his way back to his cabin, and as he walked up the verandah steps he turned back to survey the scene. There on the porch to the first slave cabin sat Pompey, eyeing him speculatively. He was not alone. By him sat another figure, dark, but unfamiliar to Simon. The white man stopped in his tracks. Seeing they were observed, the new figure quickly rose and slipped away—in the direction of the paths that led across the property. Pompey watched him go, looked at his master once more, nodded imperceptibly, then rose and went into his own cabin. Pondering this event but deciding it was no more than neighborly socializing, Simon went into the house, upstairs, and collapsed onto his own bed. He wandered all night in a fantasy world of African bodies.

Chapter Three: Rose and Thorn

Sunlight poured through the glass window into the African hut. The soft, deep, reedy voices of the natives could be heard outside as they went about their daily routines in the barn and kitchen. Simon Simmons swung his legs out of the four-poster bed and put his feet on the hard earthen floor of the hut, at the edge of the lion skin. Dark hands and limbs surrounded him, sliding over him, coaxing him back to the bed where he had rolled and lain with African flesh the whole night through. Then the grandfather clock downstairs chimed, and the hands dissolved, moving back into another world. Simon sat on the edge of his bed with his feet on the wood floor, alone, with a feeling of loss so strong it brought tears to his eyes.

Looking around, he oriented himself as well as he could to his bedroom in Mistletoe Farm, but it still seemed a little unreal, a little misty. Struggling to his feet, he staggered down the stairs and wandered into a strange room. But no, this was his dining room, and there was the son of the Chief preparing—but no, it was Toby. Wasn't it?

"Mornin' massa!" said the slim black youth, grinning broadly. "I spent the night through with Venus. We sure do get along," he said. Simon nodded and looked at him hard. Venus... wasn't she the girl from the hut by the stream, with the ripe breasts? Silently, Simon walked up close to Toby, who set down the basket of bread he was holding and stood still, eyes downcast. Simon enfolded the black slave in his arms, burying his face in the short, thick skullcap of crisp hair, smelling the clean scent, nuzzling ears and nose and lips, seeing only dark skin and bright eyes. Outside, the cry of an elephant could be heard in the distance. "Massa," sighed Toby, and tentatively clasped his master around the hips. They stood still for a long moment, and then Simon seemed to awake with a start, and looked at the purple black eighteen year old as if for the first time that morning. He gently pushed away.

"Yes, Toby. You must save yourself for Venus, and perhaps, for here, later," said Simon, rubbing his eyes. Toby looked at him in concern.

"You feels well, massa? You alright?"

"Yes, Toby, I am," he replied. "Thank you for the breakfast." He sat down and bade Toby to do the same. As with their other meals, Simon kept staring at the slave, who by now knew simply to continue eating and not question his master's scrutiny. When they were finished, Simon went outside to the privy. Emerging, he walked toward the wash house, in the door of which were Toby and Pompey, talking. Pompey cast a quick glance at the approaching white man and whispered something, then both slaves nodded toward Simon. Toby left quickly to return to the main house, while Pompey remained by the door.

"Mornin' massa," he said, "we all got started on our work already. It's a fine mornin' massa."

Simon nodded thoughtfully, looking his slave up and down. He slowly reached out a hand and laid the palm and fingers flat against Pompey's shirt front, over the thick slab of chest muscle. He held it there for a few minutes, concentrating, feeling the heat of the flesh, then removed it and looked once more at the twenty year old's face. Neither spoke, until Pompey broke the silence.

"You alright this mornin', massa?"

"Yes, Pompey, I—I had trouble waking up."

The black man nodded reflectively. "Massa, why you reckon they call this place Mistletoe Farm?"

"I don't know, Pompey," Simon said. "No doubt there is mistletoe in the trees."

"Sure, that's right, they likely is," said Pompey. "Mistletoe, that's the herb you put up high and you sit under and hope somebody come kiss you, ain't it?"

"Yes, Pompey, it is. A pleasant practice."

"Yassuh. I done heard tell of this gal, she don' wanna do nothin' but sit under the mistletoe all day. Jes' dreamin' of somebody comin' to kiss her. Seems like she sort of got lost in her thoughts sittin' there. You think that could be true, massa?" And here Pompey raised up his eyes from their customary deferential look downward to gaze intently at the white man.

"A curious tale, Pompey," said Simon, his eyes now running over the black slave's broad shoulders and muscular chest. "Curious tale—no, I doubt that it is true." Simon shook himself. "Well, I must bathe. I will be out to supervise the work a little later." And with a nod he stepped into the wash house. Pompey remained on the stoop looking thoughtfully at the door for a moment, then went off to do his work.

Simmons emerged a few minutes later, blinking in the sunlight, now fully awake. Returning to the house he dressed for the day, then began strolling around the farm. He was pleasantly surprised that his servants had begun work for the day without instructions, each taking on their appointed tasks and more. The hen house had been quickly organised, the livestock were fed, watered, and seemed clean and content. The last of the plots for a late harvest of vegetables had been sown, and Toby and Venus could be seen moving through the orchard, assessing the progress of the fruit crops, picking what was ripe. With all morning bathing complete, Aphrodite and Rose were hard at work in the wash house scrubbing clothing and linens. Gradually their handiwork began to appear on lines or flung over fragrant bushes to dry in the morning sun. In the barn, Pompey and Thorn were hard at work organizing supplies, making them accessible yet as secure as possible from the ravages of weather and vermin. Simon was surprised, but pleased, to see that the slaves had devised their own systems of organization without being directed, both here and throughout the farm. They were making the work their own.

Seeing his master, Thorn turned and grinned broadly. "Mornin' massa! We gonna get us some cats to keep the rats out!" Simon smiled and nodded in return.

"Do that, Thorn," he said. "Perhaps we can have some from neighboring farms."

With work proceeding apace outside, Simon withdrew to work indoors. He had not really inspected his new house thoroughly, from root cellar to the hot, peaked-ceiling attic, since moving in but a couple of days ago. He now inspected everything thoroughly, and brought his own records and correspondence up to date. He could do nearly all his business through the weekly delivery of supplies from Roanoke, which would also carry mail back and forth for him. Indeed, he preferred it this way, to remain at Mistletoe Farm in his own kingdom and go into town as little as possible. As he worked he heard Toby enter and leave the house from time to time as the youth performed his duties as house servant, but since there was little to do inside yet, Simon was alone for most of the day.

In the late afternoon he rose from his work and walked out to survey the work being done outside. It seemed as if the farm were growing more orderly with every hour; the people were not only performing their chores with good will and energy, but with care and responsibility as well. One might have thought that Mistletoe Farm were, in some sense, theirs from the improvements large and small they were making to its lands and buildings. Nodding with satisfaction, calling out encouragement, Simmons strolled through his property.

Walking through the vegetable plots, now prepared, sown, and waiting for rain and sun to bring up late summer crops, Simmons reached the line of trees on the far edge of the fields. Curious, he stepped through them and found, as he had surmised, a well worn path running parallel to the trees. Turning to his right, he strolled but a few yards along before he heard soft voices and the sound of feet, and in another moment he saw Thorn carrying a burlap sack, in the company of a large, muscular black man whom he did not know.

Both slaves ducked their heads in quick bows upon seeing Simmons. Thorn stepped a little ahead. "Massa," he said, "this here is Titus, he from the White Springs farm down yonder," and he pointed down the path in the direction the two had come from. Titus bowed again, saying "Massa."

Simon nodded in acknowledgement. He gazed for a moment at the dark brown face, trying to place it—and he wondered whether he was the slave who was sitting and speaking with Pompey late the previous night. Simon decided it was not worth pursuing, and then turned to Thorn. "And what have you in the sack, Thorn?" he asked.

A wide grin split the deep caramel face. "Kittens, massa, three of 'em! Titus, he gave 'em to me, they has got more than they needs at White Springs!" He held up the sack, which was undulating a little.

Titus chuckled. "It's true, massa, y'all is welcome to them, we got lots of cats."

"Thank you, and thank your master for me," said Simon. "And you Titus, have I seen you on this path before? I think many of the servants of the neighboring farms take this route, do they not?" Titus nodded, mumbling a "yassuh." "So where are you headed to now, Titus?" asked the white man.

"I is taking a ham to Ol' Mist'ess Woodruff over at Owlcroft Farm, massa, from my massa Hampton. Mist'ess Woodruff, she shore is poorly these days." Titus hefted his own burlap sack with the unmistakable heavy lump of a smoked ham inside it.

Simon nodded. "I see, I see. Perhaps one day I shall meet more of my neighbors. Well, have a pleasant journey, Titus. Thorn, perhaps you should feed these kittens and introduce them to a new home in the barn."

Half an hour later, Simon emerged from the wash house having cleaned off the day's grime, and was passing Rose and Thorn's cottage when he heard the low but unmistakable sound of an "Ow!" from inside. He stepped onto the small porch and then opened the door without knocking. Sitting at the table was Thorn, his shirt sleeves rolled up, applying a small amount of some substance to his left hand. The eighteen year old started at the unexpected sight of his master.

"Thorn, did you cry out?" asked Simon, entering and shutting the door behind him. "What is the matter?"

"They kittens done scratched me comin' outta the bag, massa," he said. "'Dite, she give me some salve to put on it, it stings a mite," he said, holding up his left hand which sported three short scratches. They did not look serious. Simon walked around behind the boy's chair to examine his hand, then released it and patted the boy's shoulders.

"I think you'll live, Thorn," he said, idly running his hands along the boy's thin but muscular shoulders and the rounded curve of the biceps. "Yassuh," murmured Thorn in reply, then sat very still and quiet as his master's hands continued to glide, and then to knead, his shoulders.

Simon's fingers slid down into the open collar of the boy's shirt, sliding over the smooth, hairless, deep caramel skin. Looking down at the very short covering of tight, black kinky hairs on the boy's scalp, Simon continued rubbing and kneading in a rhythm that seemed to take him away from that time and place.

The physical attention was beginning to have an effect on Thorn as his slim, long penis began to push out against the front of his trousers. It reminded him of an earlier promise. "Massa," he said in a low voice, "is I gonna be a breeder? You want me to breed, massa? Maybe that Venus gal?" he asked, full of hope.

By way of answer, Simon tugged on the boy's shirt, pulling it up over his head and arms, the young slave willingly complying. Pressing himself against the back of the chair, leaning forward over the seated boy, Simon rubbed the large nipples on the thin, muscular pads of the boy's chest. The slave moaned very softly, more of a whisper. "Stand up," ordered Simon.

The boy did so, and turned to face his master. Staring intently at the thin, muscular tube of the boy's torso, a deep, rich caramel color, Simon ordered the boy to turn around slowly, first this way and that. Like a puppeteer, he pulled the invisible strings of ownership to make this flesh move at his will. And then the white man, almost absentmindedly, began removing his own clothes. Thorn looked in confusion at this spectacle, then away, then back again, risking glances at his master's face to learn what it meant. Simon's shirt fell, then his trousers. "Remove those," Simon said to Thorn, nodding at the boy's own pants. Wordlessly the boy slave nodded and did so, dropping his undergarment as well, at the same time that Simon did likewise. Open-mouthed, the eighteen year old stared at the naked white man whose penis was quickly rising, fully engorged and turning redder with every passing instant. Thorn's own slim, boyish penis sprang instantly erect, curving up and away from his body above dangling balls.

In two steps Simon was on him, catching the boy up in an embrace. Thorn gasped and exclaimed "O!" He had dallied with other boys of his home plantation, and had heard of masters taking their pleasure with slaves, but this was his first physical contact with a white man. Both man and boy were lost in the experience of different skins and hair, standing tightly together, grinding their bodies into one another and hands sliding up and down and around backs and buttocks. Thorn's mouth, at chest level, licked and sucked his master's white skin and pink nipples. Their penises slapped and slid together, lubricating each other with precum.

Now breaking the embrace, Simon swept the boy's thin, naked body up in one swoop and carried him to the larger of the two beds in the room, laying him in the middle. Covering the boy's body with his own, his head over the slave's groin, Simon took the slim but iron hard penis into his mouth even as the boy, in wonder, accepted the red and purple white man's rod that was pressed down upon his own mouth. Man and boy, white and black, master and slave sucked and fondled, hips gently moving up and down to slide cocks into willing mouths.

A creak of the floorboards startled the two on the bed, and they both looked up, craning their heads around each other's bodies. There was Rose, having entered the cabin unobserved, her hand on a basket of freshly gathered field greens which she put on the table. She was staring with open-mouthed wonder at her brother and master engaged in passionate fellatio. Simon leapt from the bed, while Thorn covered his genitals ineffectually with his hands.

In two steps Simon was upon Rose, holding her in a passionate embrace by the shoulders, kissing her full lips. She gasped, still wide-eyed, her fingers splayed in the air, not knowing what to do. She was certainly not a virgin, the young girls of her home plantation having engaged in sexual play from an early age, but this kind of passion from a white master was new to her. "Strip," Simon said, taking a step back, and she willingly if warily complied in an instant, still unsure of what was to come. Her curved, muscular eighteen year old body was revealed, dark caramel skin stretched tight and oiled over small, full breasts and rounded buttocks and belly. Thorn gasped upon seeing his sister naked, although Simon knew it was not for the first time.

Taking the slave girl's hand, Simon led her to the bed and moved her into place next to her brother, who quickly scooted over, his eyes all over his sister even as he continued to cover his own nakedness. Simon lowered himself on top of the girl, his slick, leaking penis now sliding up and down her rounded belly, his hands cupping the orange sized breasts, lips and teeth tasting of shoulders and nipples and arms. In an instant, Rose was responding in like fashion, her hands clutching at her white master's back and buttocks, heedless of her naked brother lying beside her.

Simon reached down to spread the girl's legs apart and then placed the slimy head of his rigid dick at the entrance to her vagina, moving it up and down for lubrication. He gave a gentle push and she cried out. More stimulation of her clitoris with his cockhead followed, and another attempt, which seemed to bring the girl pain as well. Her eighteen year old body was not ready yet, too caught up in passion to relax sufficiently. It was the reverse situation from yesterday's experience with Venus, in which Simon had to penetrate the older girl to make room for Toby's massive penis. That strategy suggested a similar plan for today. Sitting back on his haunches and moving to the end of the bed, Simon turned to Thorn.

"Thorn, you wish to be a breeder? Then show me your work now, with your sister."

"My—my sister, massa?"

"Yes, now," the white man ordered. Thorn looked to his sister, who smiled a little and nodded, caught up as she was in the passion of the moment. It confirmed what Simon had guessed, that the two had played their own little games before this. "Yassuh" breathed the slave boy, then turned over onto his sister. Eager, she reached down to grasp his rigid, curving rod and placed it in the entrance to her vagina. Lubricated by their white master's precum, Thorn's cock now easily slid into Rose's relaxing vagina. She cried out, but now in passion rather than discomfort.

With the eagerness of a eighteen year old, Thorn began pumping his penis in and out. The boy's and girl's straining feet touched Simon's knees as he sat directly behind Thorn to watch, enjoying the sight of the boy's rounded muscular bottom rising and falling, the muscles working in rounds as they clenched and pushed in rhythm. Rose pulled her brother's thin torso down onto her small breasts and rounded girl's belly and then wrapped her legs around him to anchor the iron rod that he now plied in and out, in and out. Thorn began an animal sound, a kind of keening noise, that grew stronger and wilder until the boy threw his head up from his sister's shoulder and bellowed, clenching, his pelvis slamming forward into the girl as his orgasm flooded her vagina with semen. Shuddering and then pumping, it took several seconds for the boy to drain himself into his sister's vagina. Finished, he slumped forward. But he was not to rest there, for Simon swatted his upturned bottom with a loud smack.

"Move over," he commanded the slave boy. With a gasp, Thorn pulled his still rigid cock out of his sister. Her vagina winked open now, a smear of the black boy's white semen clearly visible. Assuming a position again with his cockhead at Rose's vagina, Simon pushed tentatively, then glided in all the way on a road of the black boy's sperm.

Rose gasped and arched her back, pushing her small rounded breasts up into the muscled chest of the white man above and inside of her. Instinctively her hands reached up to grasp Simmons around his back, then around the small of his back, pulling him down into her. Her deep caramel body writhed and she began whispering "O! Massa, O! Massa" rhythmically. Simon's hands now squeezed her breasts, now grasped her slim but muscular shoulders, his mouth tasted her puffy nipples and then again her sweaty neck and then again her full, out-turning lips. Not fast but powerfully, the white man's hips began pistoning in and out of the black slave girl while she thrashed and moaned on the bed.

Alongside them, Thorn risked first one hand and then two on his master's bottom, squatting by the two heaving buttocks, kneading and pushing the firm white hills of the man's butt as he pounded his sister's cunt. A thin line of semen still hung from the tip of the slave boy's long, dark chocolate penis. Suddenly Rose cried out frantically and began shuddering, digging her nails into the small of Simon's back: her ecstasy was upon her. Simon's speed doubled, pistoning in and out with the speed of a fan, and then he too cried out and slammed forward, grinding his pelvis against the slave girl as he shot his own semen into her vagina to mix with her brother's. White man and black girl remained clutching, writhing, gasping for another moment as the slave boy squeezed his master's tight bottom. Then the master slumped down, exhausted, draining the last of his sperm into the moaning girl beneath him.

In a sense, Simon didn't really awake from his doze of repletion for the rest of the day. From then until the next morning, there was never a moment when he was not clutching dark caramel flesh to his own tanned white body. When Thorn rose to use the chamber pot, Simon held Rose between his legs, leaning her back against his chest, fondling her breasts as she held the pot for her brother. When Rose left the bed to prepare a simple meal for the three, Simon rolled on top of Thorn and explored his mouth with his own, tongue sliding over thick, rolled lips, gliding along teeth, dancing with the black boy's tongue. Reliving childhood memories of his friend and slave Brutus, Simon sucked the black boy's stiff young penis until it shot out another load of semen into his mouth, at the same time that Rose struggled to suck and swallow from his own man's cock. When at last he slept it was with a face buried in dark, tight curls and hands on a firm brown buttock, while at his back the half erect penis of a slave boy lay against his bottom. Outside, Simon Simmons's farm echoed to the cry of giraffe, lion, and peacock. There was a faint drumming in the distance. His dreams were of a world and a continent far away.

Chapter Four: Aphrodite and Pompey

In the early morning hours Simon Simmons untangled himself from a nest of caramel brown limbs and staggered into the cool dawn light of Mistletoe Farm. For an instant a shimmer of thorn trees, savannah, drum beats, and the distant roar of lions hung in the air, more sensed than perceived, and then the veil rose to reveal the Blue Ridge foothills of his Virginia home. He shook his head to clear it and made his way to the wash house where he cleaned himself thoroughly. He walked alone back to the main house, his head full of dreams, then up to his own bedroom where he removed his clothing and went to bed naked, curled up beneath the cool sheets, slipping into distant dreams. From Toby and Venus's cabin, a dark hand which had held a curtain aside withdrew, a bright eye pulled back from monitoring the scene.

Floating back into consciousness in the late morning, Simmons looked reflectively at the bright rectangle of his window, curtains moving with the breeze of high summer. He felt—he didn't know how he felt. Torn between a world that was his and a world that was not, and unable to tell the difference. He rose and dressed, then walked downstairs and out onto the verandah to greet the day.

Toby had been trimming the boxwoods around the house; he looked up brightly as his master stood blinking in the sunlight.

"Mornin' massa! Let me get you some breakfast!" Simon smiled at him and nodded, then sat in one of the rockers, surveying the scene. Sights and sounds of activity were apparent; he marveled again at how his new servants had, in only a few days, become so involved and invested in running Mistletoe Farm. He had issued no orders for the day's activities, yet he could tell that tending of animals and gardens, washing and cooking, the gathering of firewood, were proceeding apace. Simmons gratefully acknowledged the breakfast tray that Toby brought to lay before him across the arms of the rocking chair.

Simon neared the end of his meal and was sipping coffee when he noticed out of the corner of his eye two people casually walking across the lawn, as if going from the separate kitchen to the vegetable fields. Craning forward to see, it was apparent they were two black men, and not belonging to Mistletoe Farm. In his surprise, Simmons cried out "Hallo! Hey there!" The two men, seeing they had been spotted, walked at a quicker pace to present themselves at the bottom of the verandah steps. They bowed and removed the battered slouch hats they each wore, murmuring "Massa" and "Yes, massa" as they stood before Simons.

"Who—who are you, where are you from, what is your business?" he asked them, not really knowing what to say. As he spoke, he took in their appearance. One was a man who appeared to be in his thirties, very dark, with an enormously powerful build. The ragged shirt he wore was open to the navel in front, and his dark skin stretched tightly over massive, defined muscles, oval dark nipples coming in and out of view as the shirt shifted with his movements. His neck was thick and muscular, his head pear shaped, crowned with a short cap of dense, kinky hair. His features were thick but not unpleasant; everything about him exuded strength, bulk, and masculinity. He stood nearly six and a half feet tall.

The other man was perhaps twenty and slender, a lithe, muscular but slender body inside a tobacco colored skin that shone with the morning light. His head was oval shaped, perched atop a slender neck. This young man's hair was tightly curled peppercorns dotted in thick clusters. His features were almost Asian, high cheekbones and almond eyes beneath thick, curling lashes, a generous nose but not flat, above a full rosebud mouth. He spoke first: "I is Rodney, massa," he said.

"I is Romulus," said his larger friend. "Beggin' yo pardon, massa, we is from Owlcroft, we is jes' passin' through and yo' servants gave us some water," he said, nodding toward the kitchen. At that moment, Pompey came around the corner of the verandah from the direction of the kitchen. "Yassuh, massa," Pompey said, a little out of breath in his hurry, "these is Mist'ess Woodruff's people, from Owlcroft. They jes' passin' through." He kept his head bowed but scrutinized his master from the corner of his eye.

Simon's eyes played over the two newcomers' bodies, taking in their skin tones, facial features, the contours of their bodies. As moments ticked by the scene seemed to freeze in time, the three black men waiting, furtively but steadily watching the white master—while Simon's mind occupied itself with dark oiled skin, tightly curled hair, out-turning lips and high, muscular buttocks. Then Simon's gaze seemed to snap back into focus. He nodded. "Very well, welcome to Mistletoe Farm," he said, a bit abstractedly. "You...you are welcome to the water," he murmured. The three blacks murmured "Yassuh," bowed again, and were off, each sneaking peeks back at the white man on the porch.

Simon sat a while longer in the sun, seeming to gather strength and focus. The people of Mistletoe Farm continued to go here and there, doffing caps or nodding to their master as they passed the verandah. As time went on, he finally rose, put on his hat, and set out to walk the grounds of Mistletoe, observing his servants as they went about their tasks of their own accord.

Reaching the path behind the row of trees beyond the vegetable field, Simmons decided to explore it, seeing where it might lead and which farms it might cross. He turned left and walked along, noting how well worn it was, weeds and undergrowth kept down by the frequent passage of feet. Birds cried in the summer sun and the wind stirred the trees as he made his way past fields and orchards, the hills of the Blue Ridge piled up in the near distance on his right.

He had walked no more than a mile or two when he came upon Titus, coming in his direction. "Massa," said the slave, doffing his battered hat and bowing slightly.

"Where are you off to, Titus?" Simon asked, stopping in the path.

"Back to White Springs, Massa," he replied. Simon nodded and then fell silent, looking up and down at the strong body of the slave. Then he reached out his hand and squeezed the strong arm, keeping the grip for a moment. "Very well, have a safe journey," he said. Titus nodded, but remained where he was, looking back at the white man intently as Simon passed along his way down the path. Another mile, and the path turned to follow the curves of a creek with quickly moving water. The shade and water brought some relief from the sun, which was now making the afternoon quite hot. Now fast moving, now spreading out into deep holes, the creek meandered among the farmlands. Sometimes Simmons saw a distant farmhouse on a hill, but for the most part he saw only cultivated fields, most of them tall with corn planted earlier that summer.

A distant sound became closer and louder as Simon strolled along the path by the creek. A murmur, shouts, squeals—he rounded a bend in the path and heard the unmistakable sounds of water play on the other side of a wall of tall grass and underbrush between the path and the creek. Cautiously Simmons pushed into the head-tall grass, pushing it aside to discover the source of the shouts and splashes. What he saw made him catch his breath.

In a deep pool bordered by a clay bank, three feet below the surface of the path, were perhaps half a dozen girls, naked, ranging in color from caramel to darkest brown, playing in the water. Simon quickly withdrew his head and looked to the left and right, up and down the path. Nobody was coming; indeed, Titus was the only person he had seen on the path the whole time he himself had walked it. Parting the grass, Simon looked back at the entrancing sight just a little below him.

Slippery as eels, the girls were clearly on holiday from whatever farm or plantation they belonged to. The youngest, a couple of eighteen year olds with bodies like boys, slim and taut with muscles that would soon develop into curves, splashed in the shallows on the other side of the pool. Another eighteen year old pair, deep chocolate brown, treaded water just below Simmons, firm conical breasts just at water level. Sitting on the far clay bank was a caramel brown girl of perhaps eighteen, water still glinting in her bush of jet black curls on her head, and a smaller one in her groin, her breasts large but high. Higher up on the bank just below the line of trees and brush was perhaps an eighteen year old, jet black with moderate breasts in firm, high cones that ended in pointed nipples, sunning herself, rubbing water from her shock of braided black hair.

Simmons waited a moment; still nobody else came by, and as he thought quickly it became clear to him that these girls were swimming naked here precisely because few people ever did come by this spot. He had come upon it himself quite by accident. His heart beat faster and his breath became a little strained as his eyes slid over first one young beauty and then another luscious piece of flesh. They had not detected his approach, nor had they heard the rustling of the grasses on his side through the sounds of their own voices. As if in a spell, under a powerful compulsion, Simmons found a way to step down to the level of the pool still concealed by grasses. Off the path, he shed his own clothes quickly and quietly, then, his eyes still fixed on first this then that girl slave, he pushed through the grass and stood on the slippery clay verge of the pool.

Time stopped. The two youngest stared with open mouths, seeing their first naked white man, not knowing whether to laugh or run. The other pair paddled back against the bank, their arms thrown across their swelling bosoms; they had enough experience of white males to know what could happen. The others covered their nakedness with their hands and began to scramble back up the bank as Simon waded into the pool, looking now here and now there, his reddish organ beginning to fill and rise. Then—out of the corner of his eye, was that Rodney, whom he had met earlier in the day, parting the grass on the other side of the bank? Those delicate Asian features, it must be him, whispering urgently toward the two older girls, nodding toward the white man—and then he was gone. The two girls whispered with each other and then—wonder of wonders, began to walk back down the clay bank toward the pool, and toward Simon Simmons. They in turn gestured quickly and whispered a few words to the other girls. Each of them looked sharply at Simmons, appraising him, seeming to make a decision. It happened so quickly that the white man was not sure he'd seen it. And then he was up to the youngest who stood mid-thigh deep in the water, rivulets running down their dark chocolate boyish bodies, still staring at the white man who was coming up to them.

Simmons swept up one in his arms and held her, her lithe dark body limp in his arms. Looking into her dark and shining eyes, he bent and kissed her, sucking her thick young lips into his mouth. She gasped but did not push away. Simmons's mouth moved down her thin neck to her barely swelling chest, nibbling the dark nipples on breasts like oranges, licking the water slick chocolate skin down to her navel. Now she giggled, and squirmed in his arms. The other eighteen year old looked up to her older companions for guidance. They gestured as they made their own way into the pool. Nodding, the girl still in the water grasped the white man's reddish penis with her thin brown hand, making Simon gasp and look down. He quickly set down the girl in his arms and pulled both girls toward him, his hands grasping a pair of thin black buttocks on each side. The girls giggled and now the second girl grasped his penis as well, making a game of what had been an uncertain and possibly dangerous situation.

The white man was so engrossed in the slim chocolate bodies snuggling up to him, hands slowly pumping his now rampant cock, that he did not notice the ways in which the two older girls were gesturing and whispering to their companions, seeming to direct the action as if at a play. The oldest began skirting the far edge of the pool, making their way to the far bank near where Simon now stood in the shallows, entranced, fondling the two boyish girls who squirmed and slithered against his body, giggling. One eighteen year old stayed on the bank, completely naked, watching and appraising. But the other splashed through the water toward Simon and reaching him, pressed her water slick body against his and laughed softly. Simon steadied himself in the water and then pushed back, releasing the two little girls at his side, enveloping the caramel brown girl in an embrace. His iron rod slid upright between them, sliding between their wet bodies.

Laughing again, the girl slipped from Simon's embrace and skipped through the water toward the bank, gesturing to him to follow. He was right after her. Reaching the bank she tumbled down onto its wet clay, Simon flinging himself at her side a moment later. Her firm, high breasts pointed toward the sky, large conical nipples now swelling. A fierce energy came on the white man, who seized first one and then the other breast with his hands, kneading them, and then flung himself on top of the girl's prostrate body, sinking both hands into her bush of jet black frizzy hair while he mashed his lips against her full, reddish brown mouth. Heaving on top of her body, thrusting his penis up and down on the skin of her torso, the two wrestled in that way for a while, panting, murmuring.

Then Simon became aware that the slightly older girl, the ringleader of the band of nymphs he had discovered, had slid down onto the ground next two them and was running her hands up and down their bodies.

She inserted her head with its mop of twisted braids in between brown girl and white man, kissing both, pressing her own pointed breasts into the dark body below and the white body on top.

Simon slipped up and off the girl for a moment, parting her legs, placing the full, plump cockhead of his rampant dick against her opening. Both their bodies were slick with water, with the wet clay of the bank, with their natural flowing juices. The white man pushed his rod into the black girl in one full stroke. She arched her back and cried out, but dug her fingernails into his back and pulled him into her even tighter. Arched over her now, holding himself off of her with his palms on the bank, he began pumping and banging wildly, frantically, beyond the bounds of any natural rhythm. The older girl stayed where she was alongside the couple but kept sliding her hands up and down the white flanks of the man and the caramel brown thighs of the slave girl. Master and slave, wordless until now, began murmuring and gasping incoherently, both uttering words in some strange language. On the struggle went. Then the girl climaxed, shouting out, twisting beneath the man, shuddering, her hands now flailing out to her side. It made her vagina contract, and its rhythmic pulsations brought him to the edge. Crying out as well, he slammed forward, grinding his loins down into hers as his semen poured down into the brown slave girl beneath him. Out it poured, and then the wave that had washed over him passed, and he collapsed, exhausted, onto her heaving, full breasts.

Simon drifted into a doze for a moment, then back up, pleasantly, still atop the slave girl whose breath was only just now returning to normal. He felt a tugging to the side; it was the older, dark brown girl, pulling him off of her companion. Over he came to sprawl on the bank, his penis pulling out of the slave girl with a plop. He lay on his back, the afternoon sun blinding him, breathing in deep sighs, aware only of the two warm bodies nestled on either side. Moments passed, and then the blinding sun was blocked. Regaining focus, he saw the youngest girls hovering over him.

One on each side, they crowded in over him on their hands and knees. "Massa" each whispered, then bent to kiss his ears, his forehead and nose, his neck. One offered her full mouth to his lips while another nuzzled his throat with her lips and tongue. Their firm but small breasts bobbed just over him, sometimes grazing his chest or belly. In an instant his penis began to rise again, arcing up over his thigh as it traveled toward his torso. Still the eighteen year olds kissed him, now nibbling his chest and nipples. Simon brought his hands up to fondle them in return, rubbing his hands over their rounded but small bottoms, fingers slippery with muddy clay sliding up and down the ass cracks, slipping into tight vaginas.

Suddenly he felt his penis engulfed in warmth, his thighs pressed down upon. Raising his head, he looked beyond the tobacco brown young bodies that covered his chest to see the oldest girl lowering herself onto his erect penis. He pushed his groin up to meet her, and was fully landed in an instant. Now the girl took over, sitting on her haunches over his groin, pushing herself up and down while she cupped her own breasts and looked at the white man whose rod had impaled her.

At that instant, Simon's world turned dark brown, caramel brown, tobacco brown, as both of the youngest girls and his earlier sexual conquest flung themselves onto his body as well. Every part of him was covered with a writhing slave girl, licking, fondling, biting, offering firm breasts or flat, dark nipples to be sucked. Faster and faster bounced the slave girl on his rampant dick, deeper and deeper he wandered into a world of dark beauty, clouds of tightly curled black or woven tufts, eyes both bright and dark. When he came he could hardly push up with the crush of bodies upon him. He emptied himself up like a geyser this time, in one tremendous push, and then—and then sank from consciousness, lost in a deep slumber.

"Massa!" It could have been minutes, it could have been years. Simon woke with a start. The sun must be setting, for shadows were long. He lay naked on his back, coated with streaks of muddy clay. On the far bank, standing where he once stood at the start of this adventure, was

Pompey. "Massa, you alright? I is come for you, massa," he said. Simon sat up and looked around. He was alone on the bank which was wet and roiled as if armies had struggled there. Thoughts of the afternoon came flooding back, memories—where had they gone? To whom did they belong? He shook his head, and looked once again at his own slave, waiting amidst the grass on the far side. He nodded, rose, and splashed into the water, rubbing himself until he was clean. Emerging where he had come in, he wiped himself dry, then dressed quickly and climbed back up to the path. Pompey had come down to assist him, wordlessly helping, wiping the white man's naked body dry with bundles of grass. "Thank you, Pompey," Simmons muttered. Looking to the left and right, he took a moment to orient himself. "Mistletoe thattaway, massa," said Pompey, pointing to the right. Simon nodded and set off, lost in foreign thoughts, his slave half a step behind, toward his home in the evening shadows.

At the point in the path where they turned into the trees that bordered Mistletoe Farm, Pompey gently took his master's elbow and steered him in the right direction. But as they turned, Simmons halted for a moment. A hundred yards up the path, as he was turning off of it, three dark shapes stepped onto the path from the Mistletoe grounds and slipped off farther down the path.

"Wait… who, those people, there… who were they?" he asked, unsure, thinking only that they seemed to be dark skinned.

"I didn't see nobody, massa," said Pompey quickly, then tugged at the elbow more urgently. "Come, massa, rest," he said, and they pushed through the trees, the white man too tired and wrapped up in his own thoughts to argue. The slave led his master through the vegetable fields, still furrowed from the recent planting, and toward the house. On the porches of the slave quarters and here and there in the yard were dark skinned people who eyed the two quietly as they walked up the steps of the verandah. Pausing at the top, Simmons turned around and brought the yard and outbuildings into focus. "Were there…how many people were here when we walked up?" he asked abstractedly. "Have we visitors?"

"Nah, massa, jes' the Mistletoe people," he replied, and to tell the truth Simmons could detect nobody who did not belong there now as he looked closely. Yet it seemed as if there were more but a moment before. No matter. He was tired and spent. Pompey took him into the house, there meeting Toby.

"Come on, massa," said Toby, taking over from Pompey, "I know you is tired after your afternoon, come on up to bed," he said, and led the white man to his room. There he helped his master to strip, gave him a plate with a light repast on it which he almost had to feed to him, then lifted his naked legs into the bed and put out the light. Toby had pulled the sheet up over his master and was turning to leave when a white hand reached out to grasp his forearm.

"Toby."

"Yes, massa?"

"Stay a moment. Come...come to bed. Remove your clothing, come."

Silently, Toby disrobed, the muscular contours of his slim, strong body and huge, pendulous penis visible in the ambient light. He slipped into bed beside his master and waited, still. The white man snuggled up against him, put an arm across his smooth, hairless chest, sighed deeply, then placed his other hand on the short cap of kinky hair atop the slave's head. Simon placed his own head on the dark, purple black chest and sighed again, listening to the lullaby of the strong heartbeat, breathing the clean, masculine perfume that rose from his satin skin. They lay like that for a few moments, Toby waiting and quiet, Simon moving his hands slowly over smooth skin and crisp hair. It was as Simon was drifting off in the moonlit room that he thought for a moment: how did Toby know about his afternoon? What did he mean? But he hadn't the energy to ask, and slipped into deep dreams in that moment.

Simon awoke alone in the mid morning, this time refreshed. Reaching for a pocket watch on his bedside table, he consulted the time. It was later than he thought, later than it looked. Rising, he walked naked to the window and looked out. The morning was grey, scudding clouds blocked the sun and a smell of rain came on the gusty wind. Dressing, he walked downstairs and straight out to the privy, then to the wash house where he scrubbed himself thoroughly. By the time he emerged, rain had begun to fall, a steady soaking shower, while distant thunder rolled. Sprinting to the house, he found Toby on the verandah, a brunch spread on a tray for him. He thanked Toby simply and then sat, eating, looking at the sheets of rain that moved vertically through across his view. From where he was sitting he could see the open barn door and thought he could see Thorn and Pompey at work there, moving in and out of four stalls to carry hay to the horses.

He paused. Four stalls? Four horses? They only had three. He had been glad for the initiative shown by his servants, but did it include acquiring livestock? Leaning forward he stared piercingly into the gloom of the barn, but could only see dark shapes moving back and forth at work. He turned to ask Toby, but the slave was gone, pursuing his own business. Finishing his breakfast thoughtfully, he rocked quietly. Then, as the rain began gusting onto the verandah, he withdrew, leaving the breakfast things for one servant or another to remove, and went into the house.

It was a good day to work indoors, which he did happily, continuing to put the house in order. But for the rest of the day, he sensed but never quite encountered Toby or any other slave. Going upstairs he found his bed made and room cleaned. Coming downstairs after hours of work, he found the verandah cleared and a good lunch set for him on the dining room table, but no evidence of a person who had performed that service. In the late afternoon he lit some lamps and continued his work, finally ceasing as more of the household accommodations and arrangement of his personal papers were to his liking. Still, he remained alone.

Simmons rose and put on an oilskin slicker, then walked out into the rain. It continued at the same pace, blowing a steady sheet of water. Reflecting on how beneficial that would be for the crops, he toured the place. He was hardly surprised to find nobody in the orchard or vegetable field, although there were lights in the cabins and some outbuildings. Simmons stepped to the outdoor kitchen and entered, enticed by the glow of lamplight from a window. There he found Rose and Venus.

"Afternoon, massa," they both said, each smiling pleasantly but keeping their eyes averted. He greeted them as well, then paused, his thoughts filled with the recent bouts of passion he had enjoyed with each of them. His eyes wandered over their bodies, his possessions, his to do with as he pleased. Venus broke the spell by turning to stir a pot set on the cast iron stove, and she said to him, "We is makin' a nice stew massa, you'll have some fo' your supper."

He started from out of his thoughts, then nodded and smiled. "That would be splendid, Venus. Have you... have you seen Toby?"

"He was goin' to feed the stock, massa, then see what you needed in the big house."

"Ah," he replied. "The stock. Did we... did someone acquire another horse?" The two women exchanged a quick glance. "I dunno, massa," said Rose, "that's for the menfolk, we jes' do women's work." Venus nodded agreement, but now both of them maintained a steady if furtive gaze at the white man.

"Ah... ah, I see," he said. "Well, I will ask Toby later when he brings me dinner," he said, and having no further purpose in staying there, he withdrew.

The rain had picked up, and could properly be called a storm now. Unwilling to return to the house where he had been cooped up all day, Simmons decided to walk some more, but he ended up wandering aimlessly around the grounds. Still, none of the servants were apparent outdoors. He walked as far as the orchard, and as he reached the far limit of Mistletoe the storm increased in intensity. Lightning cracked and struck nearby, a tremendous boom of thunder shaking the very ground. The wind whipped the rain above, blew up his oilskin slicker, soaking his clothes beneath in an instant. Moving horizontally, the rain seemed to find every opening in the garment and came through. Aware that he was drenched, Simmons pushed back against the wind and made his way toward the buildings of Mistletoe Farm. His head down, he hardly knew where he was headed exactly, but then saw dead ahead of him a looming structure. He made out a lighted window, and a person's figure at the window in the lamplight. Coming up to the building he realized it was one of the slave cabins, but he could not make out which. The night had come by now, brought on early by the storm. Simmons slipped around the edge of the building until he found the door. He was about to push it open when it was opened for him from inside, and so he staggered in. Once inside, the door was shut behind him and gentle hands began removing his oilcloth. Wiping the rain from his face and eyes, he looked around. He was in the cabin of Aphrodite and Pompey.

The couple stood a few feet from him, eyeing him appraisingly. They glanced at each other and exchanged a nod. They approached the dripping wet white man, still trying to orient himself after the onslaught of the storm.

"Massa, you gotta get outta those wet things," said Aphrodite, kneeling in front of him. "Let me pull off your boots."

"Massa, lean on me whilst she pulls the boots off," said Pompey softly, coming up to his master's side and putting a muscular arm around the white man's shoulders. Simon nodded and whispered a thanks. He put an arm around Pompey's thick shoulders to steady himself as Aphrodite began already to pull off his wet boots. At that, Pompey turned in a little toward Simon and put his other arm across his chest to grasp Simon's other shoulder, almost embracing him. Simon looked right into Pompey's strong, thick neck, the dark chocolate skin tones and the short bush of kinky hair. He could feel the movement of dense muscle beneath the thin layers of shirt and skin. Aphrodite tugged this way and that and first one boot and then the next came off. Without asking, she unfastened Simon's trousers and let them fall around his ankles, then tugged down his undergarments. At the same time, Pompey quickly unbuttoned the white man's shirt which was all he wore over his torso beneath the slicker, and let that drop to the floor as well. It was Simon's turn to gasp in surprise, so quickly did it happen, so quickly did he stand naked before his two slaves.

But that did not last for long. Unbuttoning her own simple garment, Aphrodite let it fall from her shoulders and stood up directly in front of Simon Simmons, the dress falling to the floor to mix with his own clothing, naked in front of the white man. Her full, taught breasts bobbed a couple of inches in front of Simon and he gasped again.

Pompey moved back and both white man and black woman stepped together in an embrace. Simon scarcely noticed as Pompey stripped off his own clothing. But he was definitely aware of the strong black man's presence when he felt him press against his back. The black twenty year old slave was covering his master's naked back even as the master pulled 'Dite into himself, grasping her firm, wide buttocks with his hands. Pompey's dick, full and iron hard but not grotesquely large as was the case for some Africans, now pressed into his master's ass cheeks. The slave's unusually large testicles mashed into the white man's upper thighs. His strong chocolate dark hands grasped his master's white shoulders and slid up and down the arms, now the sides and flanks, now around him to grasp Aphrodite and pull the three together.

In an instant Simon had surrendered himself to the flow of events, caught up in embraces front and back. Memories of every slave girl he had ever fucked came flooding back, while memories of his boyhood slave Brutus welled up in his mind as Pompey gently but insistently ground into his ass from behind. Simon began moaning, his breathing coming heavily now, his own penis pressing hard against the belly of the slave woman before him.

'Dite broke away from the embrace and, taking her master's hand, led him a few steps away to the bed. In Bulstrode's slave market the white man had taken her from behind. This evening she flung herself on her back, her legs spread and bent at the knees, and pulled the white man down onto her face to face. He followed, pushing his iron hard penis straight up between their bellies as he lay upon her, mashing her full breasts, squeezing them with his hands, finding her full lips and kneading them with his own. He tasted her, fondled her, felt the satin smoothness of her chocolate dark skin. Then, unable to delay, he pushed up off of her a little and placed the swollen head of his red penis at the entrance to her vagina. He pushed, going all the way in with one motion, while she arched her back and grunted.

Simon had no sooner landed completely inside the black girl than he felt his own buttocks being caressed by the strong dark hands of Pompey. As Simon began his rhythm of gliding in and out, he felt the black slave's fingers, slickened with some lubricant, probe his own anus. Simon's slow, preliminary movements in and out of the black girl in front created a slow in and out movement of Pompey's fingers in his bottom. And then Pompey was on him pushing up against his thighs and buttocks. Simon gasped as he felt the thick head of Pompey's purple black, iron cock press against his asshole. But the white man was powerless to stop it, caught up as he was in a dance of lust with these two people he owned as property. A searing pain tore at his butthole for an instant as Pompey pushed his way in. Simon fell forward, still fully inside of 'Dite, as Pompey pushed forward as well to mash the white man down onto the body of the slave girl. The three held that position for a moment, physically locked together. Simon's pain passed and he began slowly, tentatively, to move his hips back and forth. Pompey followed his rhythm. 'Dite supported them both.

Soon Simon was riding between two chocolate brown bodies, sliding on a sheet of sweat from their black bodies and his white one. Pompey pushed and struggled to stay landed in the white man's ass even as the white man pounded in and out, in and out of the slave girl's willing body beneath him. Hands clutched shoulders, legs and ankles locked together, fingers ran through cornsilk blonde or frizzy black hair. Pompey bit the white man's shoulders and neck as the master bit the slave girls ears and neck. Harder and faster, harder and faster, murmurs becoming cries, until Aphrodite cried out and pushed her pelvis up, her fingernails tearing at the skin of the white man implanted so tightly within her. Her orgasm clamped and jerked on Simon's pounding cock, and in an instant his own ecstasy welled up in his thighs and groin and he roared, arching downward, shooting his semen into the dark slave girl below. Feeling his partners' lust, Pompey climaxed as well, pushing forward in one massive, muscular push, holding steady as his body pinned the white man between his woman and himself. His enormous balls emptied themselves into the master's rectum, a thick and steady flow of semen filling up the white man's intestines. When he finally went limp, the weight of his muscular body collapsed downward onto the two beneath him, all three gasping for breath, heaving with the aftermath of passion.

The storm raged without while the three went through dances of passion within. Simon returned the favor to Pompey, fucking his hard, bulbuous African butt while 'Dite ran her hands over both men's bodies. Simon took Aphrodite in the rectum from behind while she crouched over Pompey, lying on his back, his penis up her cunt, both men feeling each other's hard cocks sliding through the thin wall of the slave girl's flesh between. In the middle of the night as the storm passed, exhaustion overtook them all and they fell asleep, Simon covered by dark flesh all around him, dreaming of the dark within.

Chapter Five: Good Neighbors

"Come on, now, massah," coaxed Pompey. Into the early morning light he led the smiling white man who looked around him vaguely at the yard and outbuildings of Mistletoe Farm, gathering shape from out of the dawn shadows. Simon Simmons stopped a few feet beyond the cabin door of Pompey and Aphrodite. He looked around, then shook his head as if to clear it, looked around again.

"How long... how long has it been, Pompey? How long have I...been with you and 'Dite?" he asked, abstractedly.

"Oh, three days or mo', massa, mainly in our cabin. Course, you came out to wash and use the privy, but near 'bout three days, massa."

Simon nodded again, looking around, still as if in a dream. "It seems so strange," he said. "This... forgive my asking, this is Mistletoe Farm, is it not?" Pompey nodded and murmured, "Yes, massa." Simon nodded, but remained where he was.

It was then that Pompey, who stood naked next to his master this whole time, turned slightly in toward the white man, who was wearing simple trousers and a shirt. The black man reached down to grasp the master's hand and placed it on his thick, purple black penis which hung down over his massive scrotum. Simon started and shivered, then looked down at the sight of his own hand encircling his slave's solid cock. He nodded, giving the organ a slow, gentle pump or two. "Les' go, massa," whispered Pompey, nuzzling the white man's ear through the shock of cornsilk blonde hair. One step and then two, and Pompey was leading the white man toward the privy. Simon looked straight ahead of him, one arm now around the strong chocolate brown shoulders of his slave. He spoke not a word.

In the privy, Pompey set his master on the hole and stood directly in front of him. Simon sighed, his vision taken up with the muscular hills and valleys of Pompey's strong abdomen, ripples of muscles beneath a smooth dark skin. The white man strained to urinate and to shit while he pulled the strong brown body that was his toward himself, nuzzling the black man's nipples, licking the skin below the chest...as he had done so often over the last three days. Pompey stood there, cradling his master's head in his strong hands. Then, perceiving Simon was done with his business, Pompey reached for one of the stacked corncobs nearby and, bending the white man forward, cleaned his bottom while Simon continued to press his face against the slave's abdomen, breathing in deeply the scent of his skin.

Pompey pulled the white man up, along with his trousers, and led the way from the privy to the wash house. "Take them clothes off now, massa," whispered Pompey, and Simon complied, as the slave pumped water to fill the galvanized metal tub. Gently, Pompey helped his master into the tub, helped him to sink down into the soapy water. The slave ran a bar of soap all over the white man's skin, rubbing lather into his skin, into his hair, reaching down below to clean his genitals and behind to rub his bottom, probing an inch into the rectum to make sure it was clean. Simon sat still, sometimes sighing and sometimes gasping in surprise as he felt himself grasped or touched here and there, but otherwise silent.

The sun was fully up when they were finished. Cleaned and toweled dry, Simon was led by the naked slave out into the bright morning light. By now the rest of the servants were up and about their business. Pompey made a point of pulling slightly on the white man's elbow to stop him. The slave spoke brightly: "Well, massa, everbody is up and out!"

Did Simon hear him? Probably at one level. But his sense of sight may have overwhelmed any other awareness that he had. For the people of Mistletoe Farm, his slaves, were going about their business stark naked, every one of them. "Mornin', massa!" cried Thorn cheerfully, his young penis bobbing as he walked by carrying a load of grain from the barn to the kitchen. Simon looked at him in astonishment, following the sight of his caramel brown, round, high buttocks pistoning up and down as the boy walked away from him. His vision was disrupted by Venus passing by, her high, pert breasts bobbing as she carried a bucket of water toward a cabin. "Massa!" she said, smiling cheerfully. Simon wheeled partially around to watch her go, her ample round hips swaying alluringly as she went by. The white man was not even aware of Pompey's gentle grasp of his hand, and movement of that hand to Pompey's own penis once again, so that the white and black man stood together like that, white hand around the coal black rod, watching as the naked slaves of Mistletoe paraded by.

Then Pompey broke into the moment as he pushed slightly with his hand on his master's elbow, and they started toward the house, Simon still looking to the left and the right in amazement as all the slaves of Mistletoe went by on their morning business, long and heavy dark penises swaying, full breasts bobbing, the muscles of firm, high buttocks working as they walked. Into the house they went, and Pompey led the way to the dining room. Simon sat down abstractedly in a chair at the table, looking around as if his house were unfamiliar to him; and in truth, it had been days since he had been here.

"Breakfas' right away, massa!" said Pompey cheerily, then slipped through the door behind where Simon sat. The white man was alone in the room for a moment, then heard footsteps behind him and saw a naked brown hand and arm place food and drink before him. He half turned and looked up. It was Rodney, from Owlcroft, likewise naked. His graceful head on its long neck looked down at him, a smile splitting his Asian, delicate features. Rodney's body was lithe, muscular but without the development of Pompey, or even of Toby. His body was a thin tube of meat, strong as a whip, sinuous as a snake. A nest of peppercorn curls just above his genitals matched the same pattern on his head.

"Heah somethin' to eat, massa," said Rodney, setting the plate and mug down. And then he quietly placed his own penis on the table and remained standing there. It was a beautiful organ, chocolate dark, swelling as it grew out of his body like an eggplant of flesh, prominent veins running the length of it, a lighter cockhead peeking out of a hood of foreskin. Simon could just see two large testicles hanging low in a long, pendulous scrotum sack just below the level of the table. Simon looked at his plate of greasy sausages and eggs, then down at the graceful, curved organ that simply lay on the table, inches from the plate, then back up the curved plane of Rodney's torso to his bright eyes shining above high, delicate cheekbones. "Eat, massa!" he said, and gently reached through the cornsilk hair to caress the back of the white man's neck. Simon turned to look at the knife and fork as if they were new, strange instruments. Then he picked them up and began to eat, slowly at first, then hungrily...but his glance kept flickering over to the naked black man who stood close beside him, gently rubbing his neck, softly whispering "Massa, massa" as the white man ate.

Simmons ate slowly, chewing distractedly, looking down to his side at the naked penis that lay still on the table, breathing the clean, wholesome odor of the dark chocolate body next to him. The spell was shifted, although not broken, by a sound of footsteps on his other side, and a voice: "Coffee, massa?"

Looking to that side, Simon beheld Toby laying a cup by his plate and filling it with steaming coffee from a pitcher he carried...and Toby was completely naked as well. "Toby!" Simon croaked in a hoarse voice, "why is Rodney... where did... and you, why are you naked, and why—"

By way of answer, the young man put the pitcher down on the table and then, standing as close on his side as Rodney was on the other, hefted his own huge penis and placed it on the table. Longer than Rodney's, longer and more massive than anyone's at Mistletoe, it lay like a hunk of meat, full and potent, inches from Simon's hand on that side. The white man looked down at its magnificence, lost in its fleshy heft, in the slight sheen of the skin, in the outline of the heavy cap beneath the hood of foreskin. "Massa," Toby crooned softly, "I is yo' slave. You is my massa. I do what you tells me, massa. You is my massa, suh." Toby placed his hand on his master's shoulder nearest him and began to knead it slowly, in time to Rodney's continuing massage of his neck. His eyes on Toby's penis, lulled by the soft declarations of slavery and ownership, Simon fumbled for the cup and brought it to his lips, slurping the hot liquid, his gaze transfixed on the heavy organ that lay on the table.

Was it minutes or hours that the three stayed this way, kept this tableau in place? The spell was broken by the rumbling of wheels distantly heard, then the more distinct creak of a cart outside. Rodney and Toby in an instant broke into action. Rodney pulled back the white man's chair while Toby helped his master to stand.

"Massa! our first delivery from Roanoke, massa! It been a week since we was all there!" Toby led Simon to the door, his huge penis swinging gently like the pendulum of a grandfather clock. The door opened and Pompey appeared, now fully clothed, to take his master by the arm and lead him a step or two onto the verandah. Wheeling around,

Simon looked back inside the house: both the slaves who had served him at breakfast were gone. Turning around quickly, he observed the same level of busy activity, coming and going, in the yard and buildings of Mistletoe. But wonder of wonders! every slave was fully clothed. Simon could only stand and stare. Had he imagined his earlier vision of brown and black bodies going to and fro, their naked skin shining in the morning light?

Pompey took Simon by the elbow and led him gently down the steps. As he reached the bottom, the white man was aware of quick steps coming down after him. He half turned to receive a piece of paper that was thrust into his hand.

"Massa! Here yo order fo' today, suh!" It was the eighteen year old girl from the creek, last seen pistoning up and down on Simon's erect penis as he lay in a nest of writhing, naked slave girls but three... was it just three?... days ago on the clay banks of the swimming hole. She was fully clothed. She smiled brightly, bobbed her head, and returned to the house. "Who?" muttered Simon, turning to Pompey, "How did she come to..." But the male slave did not let him finish.

"Here the men from Roanoke, massa, they has this week's order. You need to give them next week's," whispered Pompey in his master's ear, meanwhile urging him gently forward, nodding and grinning at the two rough looking white men on the bench of the wagon that two strong horses pulled into the yard.

"Mahnin', Mister Simmons," said one of them. "You... you is Mister Simmons, isn't you?"

Simon could only nod, looking left and right for brown flesh, wondering what was happening to him that morning. Pompey stepped forward a bit.

"Massa, he don' feel right this mornin', massas, but he feel better directly!" said Pompey, nodding and grinning. The two white men on

133

the wagon bench looked at the slave, then at the white man, eyed him closely, taking in his distracted look, his simple clothing. They nodded.

"Well, Mister Simmons, we got yo' order here," said the other driver. Pompey gave a barely perceptible signal and slaves appeared from left and right. Among them Titus... the tall, muscular slave from White Springs began helping to unload the wagon along with the rest. And then the huge, muscular bulk of Romulus came into view, seizing a barrel and hoisting it onto his shoulder. Open-mouthed, Simon stared after the two slaves he had seen only as passers-by before. Why were they here, how did they come to be here? He barely had time to think about it. Pompey spoke up again, addressing the two men on the wagon.

"Massa, he got an order fo' next week. It what you call a standin' order, right massa?" Pompey nudged his master. Simon nodded and looked vaguely at the sheet of paper in his hand, covered with writing and figures. Pompey prodded him gently again and he held it forward, shuffling uncertainly toward the wagon. One of the men on the bench leapt down and took the paper. He looked it over, looked closely at Simmons, then back at the paper again, then nodded.

"Yessir, we can bring these things once each week. Charge it to your account? Yes, very well sir," said the driver. Simon looked at the paper disappear into the man's pocket and tried to recall what was on it... tried to recall when he had drawn the order up.

In a few moments the wagon was empty. The drivers clucked at their horses and, as the empty wagon moved slowly from the yard, one of them called back over his shoulder, "Sure hope you feel better next time, Mister Simmons!" Simon could only nod as the wagon moved out of sight. He watched it go for a moment, then looked around the yard of Mistletoe again. Thorn, Rose, and Aphrodite stood here and there, waving in the direction of the now vanished wagon... and all three of them were as naked as the day they were born.

"Come inside now, massa," said Romulus, his huge bulk swelling up on Simon's side. The white man started as he realized that the slave was now naked, huge muscles, great lobes of chest meat, heavy hams, a thick, heavy penis all clearly visible on the muscular mountain of a man. As Romulus took Simmons by the hand Pompey simply seemed to disappear, or to slip around a corner, melting away like the morning dew... or was the white man just so distracted by the mountain of naked muscle next to him that he did not notice when or how his own slave departed?

Still enveloping the white man's hand in his enormous paw, Romulus led Simmons upstairs and into his bedroom. They stopped just inside the door. "You rest now, massa," he breathed throatily, his thick fingers unfastening the buttons on the white man's shirt, then on his trousers. Both garments slipped to the floor and Simmons stood naked before the huge black man. His eyes ran up and down the hills and valleys outlining his massive muscles. Simmons's hand was just reaching out to grasp the thick, purple black cock when Romulus scooped the white man up in one swift, sure movement. Carrying him in his arms like a new bride, he took him to the bed, where the sheets were turned back in expectation. Simon buried his face in the rolls of muscle on Romulus's chest and shoulder, nuzzling the chocolate skin that stretched smooth and hairless over the slave's hard flesh. Romulus laid the white man down and Simon reached out his arms to pull the slave down toward him... and in a flash, the huge man turned on his heel and left silently.

Simon was left sitting up in bed, his arm still outstretched, completely at a loss. Had he just imagined these slaves from neighboring farms? Had he only dreamed a vision of naked brown skin in the yard of Mistletoe? A quick pattering of feet in the hallway broke his spell of musings, and he craned his head forward to see who it might be.

It was Thorn. The eighteen year old caramel brown boy glided into the room, utterly naked. He stopped by the edge of the bed, his body a sinuous S curve of muscular flesh, the late morning light glowing on the soft sheen of his brown skin. His penis curved out over his tight package of balls, beneath a small tuft of tight curls, curved out like a dark brown flower. His rosebud thick lips were parted slightly. He spoke.

"Massa... massa, I is yo' slave. You owns me, massa. This..." and he ran his hands up and down his slim flanks, over his muscular, curving abdomen, "this be yours, massa."

Simon, stunned, transfixed, nodded, and reached out his hand, placing it on the rounded but hard belly before him. "Massa," continued the boy in a throaty whisper, "Massa, you gots to beat me, massa. Whup me, massa. Show me who the massa heah." And at that he turned around and bent over, showing his perfect, dark caramel brown, rounded bottom to his master. Hesitantly, Simon reached out again and placed his palm on the tight skin over the firm buttocks. Then he raised his hand, and then brought it down in a slap on the boy's bottom. Then again, and again. Sitting up, the white man swung his legs out over the side of the bed. Reaching out, he seized the slight frame of the black boy and swung him over his lap until the boy lay, his groin over the white man's lap, his bottom in the air, legs and torso stretched out over the bed on which Simon Simmons sat. The white man beheld the perfect hill of buttocks before him, then reared his hand back and brought it down hard on the bottom, slapping it with open palm. Thorn gasped. Again Simon spanked him, and again, Thorn gasping each time, now moaning a little. On his naked thighs and groin, Simon could feel the black boy's erection growing with each spanking. The caramel brown buttocks grew darker, a rusty purple brown hue creeping under the caramel brown skin as Simon spanked him again, then again. Finally, he pushed the boy off to stand by the bed again. His penis, now fully erect, arced out and way from his body, pointing up, a thin thread of precum dangling from it.

Thorn did not give the bedazzled white man time to plan what was next. Reaching for a pot of goose grease that was by the bed—was that here a few days ago?—Thorn reached down and began lubricating his master's penis, which began rising to full staff with that attention, and after the spanking stimulation. The white man's reddish cock rose rock hard in the black boy's hands. Reaching behind himself, Thorn rubbed some of the grease into his own rectum. Quickly, before Simon could react, Thorn threw himself over his master and onto the bed, lying on his back, pulling his knees up to his chest, spreading his thighs, baring his well-oiled anus. The white man needed no prompting. He swung around quickly and put the swollen head of his cock to the greased orifice, then pushed. Thorn cried out and arched his back as the white man slid all the way in with one push. Holding himself up off of the caramel brown body with his palms on the bed, Simon waited for the crisis to pass. In a moment Thorn nodded and whispered, "Fuck me, massa."

Completely caught up in the lustful moment, Simon began pistoning back and forth, slowly pumping, pumping. He craned his head down to taste the full, moist lips of the boy beneath him. Thorn wrapped his legs around the white man's back, locking his ankles together. Simon sucked and bit the boy's lips, licked his nose, nuzzled his bush of thick, short hair, licked and bit his neck. With every swing he pushed his penis as far into the boy as he could, the black youth grunting with the exertion. The boy's own penis stood erect between their abdomens, now slapping up against the white man's belly, now flopping down against his own brown stomach. Faster and faster Simon went, and then from far away in his thighs, his groin, his lower belly, the storm gathered, the orgasm built up steam like a distant but fast-approaching locomotive, and then it slammed through and out of Simon, pouring down into the bottom of the writhing slave boy as Simon arched his body and roared, breath seething and ragged. Clenching tightly, his whole body contracted as the orgasm washed through him, then with a mighty shudder he collapsed on top of the boy. Thorn held the white man tightly to him as his master shook and gasped while the storm passed. As Simon's breathing returned to normal, as his muscles relaxed, he slipped into a deep and dreamless sleep. As Thorn heard his regular, deep breathing, he gently rolled the white man off of him, the now limp ruddy penis pulling out of him with a plop. The white man was still asleep, and Thorn slipped from the room.

Simmons slept through that day and the next night, recovering strength. He awoke once in that time with the need to urinate. Disoriented, unsure of the time or place, he swung his legs over the bed. Instantly a pair of strong brown hands held a chamber pot for him, while another slim, coal-black hand gently grasped his penis and directed the flow. Finished, he flopped back into bed, and sleep. When he finally awoke, it was to a tremendous sense of loss that come rushing in on him. He was alone, but with a need for brown bodies that felt like a need for air.

He did not have to wait long, lying there curled up, yearning but with no plan for alleviating his lack. Toby came into the room, naked except for a simple white loincloth around his genitals and waist. "Come, massa, le's get dressed. You got to inspect the new slaves," he whispered. Confused, Simon nevertheless allowed Toby to dress him as he gazed deeply into the youth's chocolate dark skin. Toby led his master down the stairs and gave him a little to eat in the dining room. Toby stood close, his enormous penis swelling out the loincloth in plain view of the white man, as Simmons downed the simple meal. Then Toby helped him to his feet and led him outside, blinking in the sunlight, to the barn.

The center of the barn was wide, a dirt floor strewn with straw. "You sit heah, massa," said Toby, indicating a bale of hay. Simon had no sooner done so than he heard a shuffling sound. Around the corner, into the barn, came a line of black slaves, hands bound with white hemp rope behind their backs, each wearing nothing but a simple white loincloth. "These yo' new slaves, massa," whispered Toby. "They yours, they fo' you to use, massa."

Trembling, Simon stood up. He had met every one of the five slaves who now lined up before him, but he had fallen completely into the drama of the slave coffle that they were now enacting. The line of bound slaves stopped once they were inside the barn. The first two Simon recognized as the two eighteen year old girls from the creek swimming hole several days—or weeks? or years?—ago. Gleaming white loincloths covered their waists and groins, while their arms were bound behind them by white rope, their bound wrists resting on their firm, tight buttocks which already gave promise of a high, round, African shape. The girls heads were down but their small, conical breasts pointed straight out. The breasts pushed out as their arms were pulled behind them, bound behind. Their dark skin shone under a light wash of sweat and oil. Simon stepped up to them.

"What is your name?" he asked the first, "and yours," turning to the second girl. He began tugging on the loincloth of the first girl.

"I is Sheba, massa," she said, and gasped as her loincloth fell, revealing a tiny patch of curly black hair above her vagina. "I is yo' slave, massa," the eighteen year old said.

"I is Queen, massa," said the second one, whose loincloth now likewise fell to Simon's tug. "You owns me massa."

"I own your breasts," whispered Simon as he stepped up to her cupping her pert, fleshy cones. "I own your belly," he murmured as he ran one hand over the tight-skinned, muscular curve of her torso, stopping to rest in the tiny patch of pubic hair. The girl's breathing came heavier now, and she whispered, "yes, massa." Simon stepped back to the first girl and fondled her in the same way. Both were so young, just eighteen, with such promise of womanhood already. Then, his eyes lingering on them, he stepped down the line to find one of the older girls from the swimming hole next, her hands tied at the wrist behind her back, resting against her boyish bottom. Her head was down but she was grinning widely.

"What is your name?" asked Simon as he caressed her shoulders and ran his hands down her skinny arms. "Hannah, massa," she said, giggling. Simon lifted her small face under the chin and they looked into each other's eyes. In a flash he bent down and kissed her, sinking his tongue into her mouth, half-lifting her off the ground by seizing her buttocks from behind. The girl moaned and twisted but could not escape. When the white man finished possessing her mouth, her small full lipped mouth, he set her back down again. Now she looked down once more, panting, no longer grinning in play.

The white rope that went from Sheba to Queen to Hannah led on next to the huge bulk of Romulus, his hands likewise tied behind his back at the wrists. Simon stood half a head shorter than this muscular mountain of a man. He whisked the simple white loincloth off in an instant, revealing the thick, veined, purple black penis hanging over heavy, pendulous testicles. The slave was sheer beef, rolls and lobes of muscles, with no hair on his body but for a tight skullcap and a tightly coiled patch of black hair around his penis. He held his head down, his eyes focused on the ground.

Simon stepped closer to him and put the palm of his hand on the man's thick lobe of a chest. He pushed a little, moving the solid tower of muscle not a whit. He glided his hand over the hairless plane of the thick, dark chest. Simon looked over at the last slave in line; it was Titus, not as massive as Romulus but with muscles and facial features sharply etched as if testosterone were an acid, a river molding its way through the hard earth. Titus could wait, Simon thought. Then he stepped back and called, "Toby!"

"Yes, massa."

"Untie this one," he said, nodding at the eighteen year old Hannah. "Yes, massa," Toby murmured and quickly unbound the thin girl's wrists, but leaving the other slaves tied together. Simon reached out and pulled the girl over by her shoulders, placing her in the tight space between him and Romulus, facing the huge slave, her back to Simon. Hannah's eyes grew wide, staring at the powerful man's thick penis which was inches away from her at her chest level. Romulus stared impassively, curiously down at the eighteen year old girl, his eyes flickering in Simon's direction. Once his glance darted over at Titus, and Titus returned a curt nod, but Simon did not see the exchange. The white man grabbed the black girl's thin wrist and moved her hand forward, molding it part-

140

way around Romulus's penis. She giggled and grasped it eagerly; it was clear she had done this kind of thing before, and not only to Simon on the creek bank. "Pump it," Simon commanded, and she began to do so.

Standing directly behind the girl, looking down into her dark, short tangle of kinky hair, Simon held her tight by her skinny shoulders, once again running his hands up and down her arms, then around over the thin, boy's chest, tweaking her coffee-bean nipples, down onto her flat, taut belly, then back to her shoulders. Hannah, lulled by the white man's ministrations, bent to her work, her body swaying with the rhythm of her fist as it slid up and down as much of Romulus's shaft as it could encircle. The huge black man seemed to brace himself, his wrists still bound behind him, looking without expression at the thin black girl in front of him, but his breathing was now coming faster and harder. In another minute small specks of clear precum began flying out of his penis as, iron hard, the little black girl continued to beat it with a sense of purpose. Simon's gaze ran back and forth from the thin girl he fondled to the massive black slave the girl was masturbating. Suddenly, without warning, Romulus gave a grunt and then a deep, intense rumble in his chest and throat. Without ceremony, he pushed his groin forward and shot great ropes and dollops of semen straight out onto the smooth, dark chocolate body of the eighteen year old girl before him. Hannah giggled again and slowed her pace, then stopped entirely as the semen stopped flowing from the thick, hot, pulsating cock in her hand. She dropped the organ and stood still, waiting. Simon reached over and around her, seeing the great drops and streams of white semen on her dark body. He began smearing it, on her boyish chest and thin, nubby nipples, down onto her belly, making her torso shine with Romulus's copious semen. Hannah giggled again, watching the white man's handiwork. It was when Simon reached even farther and pushed a dollop of semen into the girl's hairless, unsuspecting vagina that she winced, crying out. But the semen was lubrication for the white man's finger, and it went in up to the first knuckle. Simon gave thought to the black man's sperm now swimming in the virgin canal of the young girl, smiled, and wiped his hands on Hannah's back and rounded buttocks.

He pushed her away, commanding Toby, "Secure her again." Toby did so as Simon moved on to the last slave, Titus.

Muscular but not bulky, Titus stood lean, chiseled, as if he had been hewn from ebony. Unlike most of the other male blacks, he had a diamond of tiny peppercorn tufts of hair in the center of his chest that narrowed and traveled down his abdomen to bloom again in a full bush of tight peppercorns around a heavy, full, unusually thick penis that curved out and over heavy, low-hanging testicles. He stood still with his head down. Simon walked around him to the back, then to the front, then back again. The slave's muscular arms were tied by the wrist, resting now on his firm, high, slab-sided buttocks. Simon stood behind the black man and began kneading the buttocks, digging deep into the hard muscle. Titus's fingers twitched but he did not move or cry out as the white man dug into the muscle of his butt cheeks, pressing in to push against bone. Stepping back, Simon hauled his arm back and brought it down in a tremendous smack on the bottom, then again and again. Then he walked around to the front of Titus. The black slave's penis, perhaps against his will, was semi-erect, beginning to arc out and to the left. Simon nodded and smiled.

The white man turned to Toby: "Take them into the big house and put them in my bedroom. Release them there," he said. Toby murmured "Yes, massa," and led the five blacks away in a line, hands still bound by the rope that connected them.

Simon watched them go, then walked to the privy to relieve himself. Then to the wash house, where he cleaned himself completely. Emerging into the sunlight, he looked around him—but was he seeing Mistletoe Farm? Head high, he strode resolutely toward his house: Up the verandah, up the stairs, and then into his room.

He had a momentary sense of disorientation. Nearly all the furniture had been removed. What remained was a carpet of mattresses, featherbeds put side by side to cover the entire floor. The whole room had become a bed. A pot of goose grease lay to one side of the room.

Standing quietly, watchfully, on the featherbeds were the five slaves from the barn, the females clustered together, Titus and Romulus against another wall. None of the Mistletoe slaves were apparent, nor had he seen any of them in crossing the yard. Simon lowered his head like a lion before the charge, his eyes sweeping over the "new slaves." Frantically, he tore off his clothing, soon standing as naked as the blacks were, on the featherbed carpet. Walking up to them he moved slowly from one end of their line to the other, looking at them, now and then reaching out to touch an arm, cup a breast, or lift a penis tip with just a finger. Then he seemed to make a decision and to focus. By then, his own penis was nearly erect, a long, thick shaft of reddish flesh—although no match for most of the black organs to be found on Mistletoe.

His cock swinging, rising, Simon pointed to Romulus. "You, on your hands and knees here," he said, then pointed to the featherbed. Romulus darted a quick, questioning look at Titus; had Simon been able to see it, he would have made it out to be a look of protest. But Titus nodded and whispered something sharply under his breath. Slowly, the massive black slave came closer to Simon, looked at the featherbed, looked at the white man, sighed deeply, and dropped to his hands and knees.

Simon slipped down behind the massive slave on his knees. Two hard, huge buttocks presented themselves, a sweat-shining ass creek between, and a black-brown starfish of an anus in between. Reaching for the goose grease, Simon slicked up his own penis, still rampant and now rock-hard, and then stuck first one and then two fingers into the big slave's bottom. Romulus grunted and braced himself, knees and elbows on the floor, head down, preparing for the onslaught. Simon placed the fleshy head of his cock against the anus and pushed. Romulus cried out. He pushed again, and just the head popped in. Seething, Romulus put his head down and clenched his hands. Inch by inch Simon worked his way in, while Romulus wept and moaned, surprisingly so for so large a man. Was he unused to this treatment, in contrast to the other male slaves Simon had fucked? It took a couple of minutes to be fully landed inside Romulus. Simon only grew harder and more turgid during this time, his cock achingly hard inside the soft, warm anus of the black slave before him. Completely inside, Simon began moving in and out, slowly at first and then with more energy, enjoying the sight of his reddish pink shaft sliding in and out of the dark chocolate bottom of the slave in front of him. His white thighs and scrotum banged against the hard, solid body crouched before him.

Fully into his rhythm, Simon beckoned Titus to come over. Uncertainly, the chiseled hard masculine slave approached. Simon beckoned him into place at Romulus's other end. Uncertain at first, and then grasping what was wanted, Titus planted himself on his knees in front of Romulus's head. He reached down and gently brought the huge slave's head up, whispering to him. Romulus, breathing heavily with the rhythm of Simon's pistoning in and out of his ass, raised his head and, at Simon's and Titus's direction, craned his head forward. He picked up Titus's dick with his lips, the rod growing ever longer and harder, took it in his mouth and then swallowed it.

The mountain of black flesh that was Romulus was now being fucked by the white man on one side, and face-fucked by his fellow slave, Titus on the other. Stoically, he braced himself in the middle to receive both ministrations. Simon, when not following the movement of his own dick in and out of Romulus, looked directly across the broad, muscular back at Titus, in a similar position on the other end of the slave, his dick going in and out of Romulus's mouth. Simon caught Titus's eye and, greatly daring, the slave held the gaze, the two men locked in a shared experience across the back of the large man who was giving them both such pleasure.

Suddenly, Simon's gaze was blocked. Hannah, the eighteen year old girl, had leapt onto Romulus's buttocks, straddling both them and the white man who was fucking the black slave rhythmically. Giggling, she faced Simon and wrapped her skinny legs around his back. Pulling him forward with her arms, she pulled his face into hers, greedily seeking a repeat of the deep kiss she had experienced for the first time only a few minutes before, seeking his white man's thin lips with her small, rosebud, full lips. Simon pulled the thin girl slave into himself, kissing her passionately, devouring her eighteen year old mouth and lips, as she pulled herself tightly into him.

In a flash, the most extraordinary thing happened. Building in his thighs, buttocks, and loins, Simon's orgasm came on like a powerful engine. When it blasted forward out of his dick and into Romulus, it took Simon with it. Shooting sperm directly into the big slave's ass, Simon's whole being moved forward, into the kneeling Romulus, into Hannah, through Romulus's submissive body and into Titus, who was spouting his own orgasm now into the mouth of Romulus. Slamming forward, crying one last cry on the earth, Simon's whole being moved foward into dark brown skin, kinky hair, firm and muscular bodies. Hannah squealed with the intensity with which she was held as she rode Romulus's well-fucked hips, pulled hard into Simon's bucking abdomen.

Simon went away into another world for some time, and came back to himself an hour or so later as two eighteen year old brown girls rolled him over on top of them. Entering first one, who arched her back and cried out but held on to the white man with her hands, and then the other, who winced and moaned but braced her feet against the featherbed and took the master inside of her entirely, Simon fucked first the one and then the other. Biting, licking, sucking one set of small, pointed breasts and then another, Simon pulled out of one and pushed into another, then reversed, back and forth for what must have been an hour more. By chance he was deep inside Sheba when he came, bellowing, melting down into her as his semen flowed down, merging with her flesh as he had with Romulus, Hannah, and Titus, vanishing into brown as his white fluid pumped out.

....

A little less than a week later, a wagon rolled into the yard of Mistletoe Farms. Toby, dressed in a respectable set of livery clothing, came out to greet the two white drivers and the heavily laden wagon drawn by two horses.

"Mister Simmons here?" inquired one driver.

"Naw suh, he still a little porely, but he leave this heah order for next time. He call it a standin' order," said Toby, smiling, looking down, shuffling his feet, and handing the driver a sheet of paper. The driver read it, grunted, showed it to his companion, then looked hard at Toby.

"Alright," he said, "sorry yore master ain't feelin' right. I 'member from last week. Y'all come take all this away," he said, waving at the heavy load of food, clothing, shoes, farm implements, liquor—and firearms. From around the side of buildings several slaves emerged to unload the wagon, and in a wink it was empty. The white driver looked again at the order for next week—indeed, it was a signed order for standard weekly deliveries—folded it and put it into his breast pocket, clucked at the horses and pulled slowly away. Several eyes saw him do that.

From behind curtains in an upstairs bedroom, Simon Simmons looked down at an angle, furtively. As soon as the wagon was out of sight, two brown arms reached across his naked chest and abdomen and pulled him away from the window. He went, smiling.

In the downstairs parlor, a man dressed as a Virginia country gentleman released the curtain he had pulled partially aside so as to view the spectacle of the wagon and its delivery. The well dressed man turned to his guest who sat at a desk, smoking a cigar.

"They accepted it," said Pompey. "Well done, your skills have come in handy. Once you have taught the rest of us, I hope we can all do as well."

Titus tapped the cigar against the ashtray and nodded, flicking a spot of ash off of his frock coat. "Each one teach one, as they say. The Mistletoe people are making great progress in learning. That, I think, was part of our bargain?" Pompey grinned and nodded. Titus continued: "I think I have a shift in the bedroom upstairs tomorrow at noon. Well, a small price for what we have gained, I suppose." His companion nodded.

"Tell me," said Titus, "how you knew that 'Master' Simmons would break as he did?"

Pompey sat down in an easy chair next to Titus, took up a china cup of coffee, and considered carefully. In a moment, he turned to the visitor and conspirator from White Springs and replied.

"I think all white folks might go that way. You spend yo' whole day thinking about color, worrying about it—well, that ain't no different from spending yo' whole day dreaming about color, 'bout how we look—like the world he caught up in now." Titus nodded, and bade him continue. "I could tell from the start that Master Simon could be caught up in thinkin' too hard about this, just like anybody can 'bout what interests them the most. Only thing, this was to our advantage. I think," he said, reaching for a cigar of his own out of the box newly delivered, "I think mebbe Master Simon jes' sat too long 'neath the Misteltoe."

ABOUT THE AUTHOR

Lance Kyle is a professor in a large university in the southern USA. This is his first book with NazcaPlains.